"You must take me as you find me, Mr. Jones."

Kate's chin tilted upward as she spoke.

"And you," Chester Jones said, cupping her face in his hands, "I find adorable."

"Please," she whispered, "don't play games with me."

"I never play games, Kate." He spoke intently and in a moment had taken her in his arms and kissed her.

So unexpected was his embrace that at first Kate made no move to stop him, and then she tried to push him away, her senses uncomfortably stirred by the desire she felt in his taut body. Then as if paralyzed by his touch, she ceased struggling and soon was blissfully drowning beneath his gentle caresses; his tenderness tantalizing her, exciting her beyond endurance until her body trembled violently against his and her mouth parted eagerly to receive his kiss.

WELCOME
TO THE WONDERFUL WORLD
OF *Harlequin Romances*

Interesting, informative and entertaining, each Harlequin Romance portrays an appealing and original love story. With a varied array of settings, we may lure you on an African safari, to a quaint Welsh village, or an exotic Riviera location—anywhere and everywhere that adventurous men and women fall in love.

As publishers of Harlequin Romances, we're extremely proud of our books. Since 1949, Harlequin Enterprises has built its publishing reputation on the solid base of quality and originality. Our stories are the most popular paperback romances sold in North America; every month, six new titles are released and sold at nearly every book-selling store in Canada and **the** United States.

A free catalog listing all Harlequin Romances can be yours by writing to the

HARLEQUIN READER SERVICE,
(In the U.S.) 1440 South Priest Drive, Tempe, AZ 85281
(In Canada) Stratford, Ontario, N5A 6W2

We sincerely hope you enjoy reading this Harlequin Romance.

Yours truly,

THE PUBLISHERS
Harlequin Romances

Suspicion

Jo Sullivan

Harlequin Books

TORONTO • NEW YORK • LOS ANGELES • LONDON
AMSTERDAM • PARIS • SYDNEY • HAMBURG
STOCKHOLM • ATHENS • TOKYO • MILAN

Original hardcover edition published in 1982
by Mills & Boon Limited

ISBN 0-373-02544-0

Harlequin Romance first edition April 1983

CHAPTER ONE

IT was Friday—Friday the thirteenth. Unlucky for some. Lucky for Kate Whelan. She was returning from her first business trip abroad as a fashion buyer, and Paris had exceeded all expectations. Now, as the airport bus raced along the M4, she sat looking out at the bleak English landscape. Green fields lay beneath torrential rain, giving way to dark, dismal buildings, as far as the eye could see. Cars speeding alongside, their lights shimmering in the heavy rain. Here and there life was to be glimpsed huddled beneath a dripping umbrella or an upturned collar, but the incessant downpour encouraged few loiterers. Kate lay back in her seat and closed her eyes, a smile hovering about her lips; Paris was too recent an experience for any of this to be of consequence.

She had worked on the fashion floor of Bennett's department store for several years, but a keen mind and a capacity for hard work had advanced her steadily in an upward direction, until she was now part of the central buying team; responsible for the merchandise of one of England's largest retailing groups. Mindful of her good fortune to be doing a job she loved in such friendly surroundings, she smiled at the thought of her initial reluctance to accept promotion.

Their bus had gradually reduced its speed as it left the suburbs behind and reached central London, and now, caught up in the evening rush hour, had come to a standstill. Up till then Kate had hardly noticed the slim, dark-haired girl seated opposite, but as the bus lurched suddenly forward, she opened her eyes and caught the girl's intent stare. The latter hesitated for a moment, then leaned forward.

'Please don't think me rude, but do you work for Bennett's?'

Kate looked perplexed. 'Yes ... yes, I do. I'm the sportswear buyer. But how ...?'

'I saw you with the other buyers at the airport.'

'I see,' said Kate, not really seeing.

The girl's eyes strayed to the window and there was a moment's silence before she blurted out: 'I *used* to be the sportswear buyer at Bennett's.'

Kate gave a smile of recognition. 'You must be Joanna Hill. I'm sorry, I didn't recognise you.'

The girl raised her hand to her wet hair. 'I'm not surprised—I must look a fright. The rain simply fell out of the sky and I didn't have my umbrella.'

'As a matter of fact you left one in the office. One of the girls put it somewhere safe in case you called back.'

Joanna glanced at her wristwatch. 'I suppose it's too late to collect it this evening ...'

'I'm having to go back to the office to complete a report, if you like we could share a taxi?' said Kate.

'If you're sure it's no bother?'

'Not at all,' Kate assured her. 'It's nice having company.' For the first time she noticed the girl's navy uniform. 'Are you working at the airport?'

'As a ground hostess. My German's a bit rusty, but I speak French fluently.'

'Sounds interesting.'

She shrugged and gave a half smile. 'It gets me up of a morning ... I don't believe we've met before. Are you new?'

'Oh, no. I worked on the sales floor, but when you left they were desperate to fill the vacancy ...' Kate flushed, silently cursing her loose tongue. 'I'm sorry, I didn't mean that to sound ...'

'Don't worry, I've long recovered. The rag trade, like nature, deplores a vacuum.' She pushed her hair back from her forehead. 'Are they keeping you busy?'

'I feel as if I'm in training for the pentathlon,' Kate confessed.

'It's that bad?'

'It's that good! Everything is so new and exciting.'

'The smell of the greasepaint and the roar of the crowd?'

Kate laughed. 'Something like that. Although it's disconcerting, suddenly having the world beat a path to your door because of your buying power.'

'Fashion journalists wanting to know your "story"?'

'My *story*?' Kate shook her head. 'Nothing so glamorous, I'm afraid. Just a never-ending queue of reps.'

'You haven't met Simon, then? Simon Forrest.'

Kate frowned. Simon Forrest wrote a prestigious column in a highbrow Sunday paper. 'No, I don't think so ... but then Publicity Department would probably deal with the Press.'

Joanna smiled ruefully. 'If publicity is all they want.'

The buying offices seemed oddly silent after the day's rush. An element of unreality hung about the dark, empty rooms, while several floors below Oxford Street, with its spectacular window displays and surging commuters, was all brightness and life. The umbrella had been well hidden, but they eventually located it in a small cupboard in Kate's room and Joanna expressed her thanks. 'It was a gift from my godmother. I would have hated losing it.' She looked about the office. 'Things don't seem to have changed much.'

'More's the pity. This typewriter wouldn't even pass an M.O.T.'

'Don't knock it. It will probably outlast both of us,' said Joanna, with a note of bravado.

'You sound as if you might be missing it all?'

She was silent, thinking about. 'I didn't think so until

now . . .' She attempted a smile. 'I suppose you know my "story"?'

'No, I don't . . .' Kate had heard surprisingly little about her predecessor, and the other buyers' studied avoidance of the subject had aroused her curiosity. 'Perhaps *you'd* like to tell me,' Kate gently asked.

There was no response. Joanna apparently didn't hear or wasn't listening. She was intently fingering a wet glove and when she looked up her eyes were brimming with tears. 'Let's just say that as a buyer I was a good judge of clothes, but a poor judge of character.'

'Was that so terrible?'

'Somebody thought so, because now you're that side of the desk and I'm this side . . .' At Kate's look of concern, she shrugged slightly. 'Don't worry on my account. For me the worst is over. For you it's just beginning.'

She stood waiting for the lift, a silent and dejected figure, watching the floor lights flicker on the indicator. After a while the doors slid open and she stepped forward, then hesitated, and Kate heard a man's surprised voice.

'Joanna! What on earth are you doing here?'

'It was raining . . . I came for my umbrella.'

'But you're wet through,' he said more gently. 'Why didn't you let me know you were here?'

'I didn't want to bother you.'

He emerged from the lift, his back towards Kate, but although he spoke quietly there was no doubting the concern in his voice.

'My car's downstairs. Let me take you home.'

Kate did not hear Joanna's reply, but she appeared not to have the emotional strength to argue as he laid an arm about her shoulders and drew her into the lift. As the doors closed, Kate stood looking after them with a thoughtful expression.

Kate was remembering this scene the next morning, as

she walked through the revolving door of the buying offices and took a lift to the fourth floor. Strange to think she had worked in the buying department for several months and yet Joanna Hill's name had scarcely been mentioned. Almost as if the buyers had closed ranks over her sudden dismissal. Elsewhere there had been a modicum of rumour and head-shaking, but the true nature of the scandal had never filtered through to the sales floor.

She sat down at her desk and pushed her fair hair away from her face. It was a golden fairness with natural highlights, that never failed to draw male glances. It fell in a straight line to her shoulders, smooth as silk; a sophisticated style that accentuated her high cheekbones and complemented her air of serenity. And yet a tiptilted nose, a large, well shaped mouth and wide blue eyes that glowed when she was happy revealed the sophistication to be only apparent. Her style of dress was simple and chic, and reflected her own femininity rather than seasonal fads and fancies. When Kate entered a room, it was her shapely figure men noticed and not the clothes she wore, a rare occurrence in the fashion industry.

Her physical well-being contrasted dramatically with the sad figure of Joanna Hill. Unhappiness had left its imprint on the girl's delicate features, and Kate wondered wistfully what had brought about such misfortune.

For the rest of the morning a rush of appointments kept her too busy to think of anything except work, but at one o'clock she had promised to meet Molly Cunningham for Saturday lunch at Parsons. Molly was senior separates' buyer at Bennett's; a stimulating red-head in her late forties, who invariably chainsmoked her way through meetings and crises, but who nurtured a sharp mind, honed finely over the years by experience and common sense. In a business noted for its fatalities and fools, Molly had survived with her reputation intact. As sportswear buyer, Kate was her direct responsibility, and it was under her skilful supervision that Kate's natural talents had first begun to acquire style and direction.

Parsons was the local wine bar that served the rag trade with drink and gossip, and as usual trade was brisk, but Molly had managed to find an empty table.

'It's bad for business,' she joked, handing Kate a chilled glass of white wine instead of her requested Perrier. 'Never let the trade think you can't handle your liquor.'

'Perhaps I do need something a little stronger,' smiled Kate. 'I ache from head to foot.'

Molly lit a cigarette and blew out the match. 'An occupational hazard, I'm afraid. Someone once made the observation that buying is ten per cent inspiration and ninety per cent perspiration.'

'Wasn't that genius?'

'Comes to the same thing in the end.' Molly took a couple of sips from her drink. 'How was Paris?'

'Very French. Very chic. I came home wanting to throw out all my wardrobe and start again.'

Molly nodded despondently. 'I know just what you mean. That's the way it got me for the first ten years, and then the money ran out.'

'I'm also very exhausted, but I'm due a week's leave on Monday.'

'Well, don't forget that on their first trip abroad buyers have to make a written report to the Director of Buying.'

'It's already done and in my OUT tray,' said Kate in a satisfied tone.

'Then pull it out. You have to present it to Chester Jones personally.'

'Oh, no!'

'Oh, yes!' Molly flicked her ash in the general direction of the ash tray. 'Don't worry, he won't bite you.'

But despite Molly's reassurance, Kate remained un-

convinced; the memory of the previous evening still clear
in her mind. Joanna had been no walking advertisement
for good management relationships. She paused, thinking better of saying what was in her mind, then said
tentatively: 'I met Joanna Hill on my way home . . .'

'Joanna?' Molly set her glass down upon the table.
'What was she doing in Paris?'

'Not in Paris, at the airport. She's working at
Heathrow.'

'How was she?' Molly asked quietly.

'Not in the best of spirits.'

'She did promise to keep in touch, but I've heard
nothing . . .' Molly hesitated for a moment, then said:
'Perhaps I should explain about Joanna.'

'Please,' protested Kate, 'don't feel you owe me any
explanation.'

'No, for Joanna's sake it's only fair to clear the air,
and besides, facts are so easily distorted by gossip.'
Molly sipped her drink. 'As you know, at the beginning
of each season a buyer is given a specific amount of
purchasing power and it's part—a very important part—
of that buyer's responsibility to stay within her budget.
To cut a long sad story short, Joanna heavily overspent
with one particular manufacturer. When his garments
failed to sell, she hid the orders and started juggling her
figures.'

'Is that possible?'

'Not now, but apparently then the system wasn't
infallible. Anyhow, when the manufacturer began to
demand payment, she started to take from Peter to pay
Paul.'

'But I thought payment of invoices was the
responsibility of the Accounts Department?'

'She juggled with figures on paper, not with actual
money. Eventually someone shouted very loudly who
wasn't getting paid and the whole affair came to light.'

'She didn't seem the type to indulge in dishonest

intrigue . . .' said Kate in disbelief.'

'She wasn't, but others were, and she got caught up in the middle.'

'No wonder she sounded so bitter last night!'

'If only she'd gone to Chester in the beginning and not panicked. She's certainly not the first buyer to have overspent.' Molly studied her drink. 'Unfortunately, Joanna allowed her personal feelings to encroach upon her professional liability. A good buyer buys with her head, not her heart.'

Suddenly out of the lunchtime crowd a young man appeared, waving a glass in one hand and a cigar in the other. 'Molly darling,' he cried, 'where have you been hiding yourself?'

'Hello, Simon.' There was nothing offensive in the quiet politeness of the words, but the tone of her voice was deadly in its contempt.

He hadn't appeared to notice. 'I hope you aren't corrupting the next generation of buyers, but if you are, may I join you?'

Molly reached for the ashtray and put out her cigarette. 'I'll see you later, Kate. I have some paperwork to catch up on.'

CHAPTER TWO

THE intruder, in his late twenties, dressed well and looked the picture of a successful young man. Kate wondered what he had done to earn Molly's so obvious disfavour.

'Hello,' he smiled, easing himself into the vacant chair beside her and signalling for a further round of drinks.

'I'm not sure that I have the time,' murmured Kate, making a movement to rise.

'Five minutes won't hurt,' he said authoritatively, 'after all, it is Saturday. And you could always say you were doing business.'

'Business?'

He tapped ash off his cigar. 'For my sins, I write for the *Sunday Dispatch*. My name's Simon Forrest.'

Simon Forrest! The only male in a clutch of fashion writers and another question mark in the Joanna Hill mystery. Kate pulled a face. 'A power to be reckoned with.'

'I'm glad somebody is impressed.'

'Molly isn't.'

He shrugged a noncommital shoulder. 'I don't let it keep me awake at night.' He reached in front of him and took both Kate's hands in his. 'Maybe you could slip in a good word for me once in a while?'

'You think it would do any good?'

He smiled. 'None at all, but I rather like the idea of a beautiful blonde coming to my defence.' He leant back in his chair and stretched out his legs. 'I take it you work with Molly?'

Kate introduced herself. 'I'm the new sportswear buyer.'

'Of course!' He leant forward with a smile of recognition. 'Now I remember. Your reputation has already preceded you.' Kate looked puzzled. 'Your photograph . . . in the *Draper's Weekly*.'

Her face melted into comprehension. She had forgotten that buying appointments were officially published in the trade newspaper. She smiled. 'I'm glad you approve.'

'I always approve of beautiful women. My column is entirely dependent upon their whims and fancies. Pleasing them keeps me in business.'

'Whims and fancies? For a business involving millions of pounds you make it sound something of a fragile arrangement!'

'Isn't it? Fortunes have been made on a hem length, on a colour. Others have lost a fortune.'

'I suppose *high* fashion has always been a gamble,' Kate agreed philosophically.

'Our mistake is believing we're in the business of selling clothes to women.'

'Aren't we?'

'We're in the business of *pleasing* them, and that's always been a high risk area.'

'You make it all sound like very hard work,' she commented. 'No wonder my predecessor up and left.'

For a moment, his intense scrutiny made her feel uneasy. 'Joanna? Do you know Joanna?'

Kate shook her head. 'She left before I took over, but she came into the office yesterday to collect her umbrella.'

His eyes flickered imperceptibly. 'She's back . . . in London?'

'Has she been away?'

'Abroad . . . Switzerland.'

In the silence that followed, Kate's curiosity got the better of her. 'Did you know her very well?' she asked softly.

'We had professional dealings. In my job I can't afford not to know all the buyers.' Simon Forrest juggled the ice in his drink. 'She was quite a sweetie . . . Too nice for this business.' He drained his drink and called for their waiter. After he had settled the bill he hesitated for a moment, then appeared to come to a decision. 'I'm short on ideas for my next column. Perhaps you could help me?'

'How?'

'Let me have a browse through your current stock. Maybe choose a couple of outfits to quote for next weekend.' His voice took on a persuasive tone. 'It could bring some extra business your way.'

Kate did not hesitate. She knew that an editorial in the right newspaper could have more pulling power than a full-page advertisement. And Simon Forrest worked for the right newspaper.

They arrived at Bennett's and took the lift to the first floor. As they approached the sportswear section Simon's eyes glanced professionally round the department. After the amorphous muddle of the other departments, the contrast in styles was dramatic. Decor was of the very plainest; lacquer red was the predominant colour for fixtures and fittings, sharply contrasting with a vast expanse of white. An illusion of space and well-being pervaded the whole department. In one corner a small bar offered a selection of fruit juices, while attractive young ladies in crisp white cotton offered smiling assistance. Tennis, cricket, golf . . . traditional outfits for every sporting occasion hung alongside sportswear of a more ambiguous nature, a more vivid hue: tracksuits and T-shirts, leotards and leggings, baggy bermudas and satin shorts, in a variety of shapes and sizes, every colour of the paintbox.

Simon blew a silent whistle. 'Very impressive! Who'd have thought women's sportswear could have such style?'

'We've come a long way from "jolly hockey sticks",
I'll have you know!'

'And gym mistresses with red noses and hefty thighs
shouting encouragement to girls in green knickers.'

Kate shuddered, 'Don't remind me, those days are
far behind.'

'I'm not so sure. I've a sneaking suspicion some of
those gym mistresses became sales ladies at Bennett's.'

Kate giggled and waved her hand around the department. 'Feel free, but let me know what styles you choose.
I have to make certain there's sufficient stock to back
up an editorial.'

He smiled his thanks and wandered off to make a
choice. Kate frowned. He appeared affable enough, and
yet she was not entirely reassured, wondering how he
had come to make an enemy of Molly. She supposed
that editing an influential column meant stepping on a
few toes.

After a week's holiday at her parents' home in the
country, Kate returned to work refreshed and quietly
pleased at her impressive editorial in the *Sunday Dispatch*.
Doubts she might have had about Simon Forrest's personal appeal, but there was no doubting his ability to
tell a story in print. She felt sure the feature would bring
about a substantial increase in trade and that Chester
Jones would approve of her public relations. On the way
to her office, several workmates congratulated her on
the Sunday article. People liked Kate. Her bright smile
and warm manner drew forth confidences as well as
admiration and few resented her her success.

Surprised not to see Molly in the office, Kate found a
message on her desk saying she was visiting their
Richmond branch that morning and would she deal with
any urgent matters that might arise. Kate spent most of
the morning visiting several manufacturers and a fabric
house, and by the time she got back to the office Molly

had still not returned, but someone else was sitting at her desk.

'Can I help you?'

The tall, dark-haired man stood up. 'I was looking for Miss Cunningham. Is she about?'

'I'm afraid not.' Kate glanced at the office wall clock. 'She shouldn't be too long. She has an appointment with Mr Jones at twelve-thirty.'

'Then I'll wait a few more minutes.'

Almost Slavic in appearance, with dark eyes and high cheekbones, the newcomer appeared vaguely familiar, and Kate wondered if their paths might have crossed socially. He was undeniably handsome, but something about his manner puzzled Kate; there was a quality of self-assurance that belied his youthful appearance, and she wondered what his business might be with Molly. As he stood looking out of the window she tried to concentrate on a report that required her signature, but after a while she became conscious of him eyeing her.

'You're new here, aren't you?' he enquired affably.

'Does it show that much?'

For some reason his presence had unnerved her and a frown flitted across her face as she looked up from her report, but he smiled back at her, reassuring her: 'No need to get anxious, I've simply been hearing about you from Miss Cunningham.'

'Nothing bad, I hope?'

'On the contrary, she has a very high opinion of the new sportswear buyer.' He looked at her in a considering way and appeared to approve. 'Miss Whelan, isn't it?' She nodded. 'How are you finding it so far, exhausting?'

'Exhilarating is more the word I'd choose.'

'As in a cold shower or a glass of Dom Perignon?'

She smiled, encouraged by his sympathetic manner and warm brown eyes. 'A bit of both, I suppose. Considering my lack of experience most people have

been very helpful and patient, not at all the ogres some
of them were made out to be.'

'I'm not surprised. You're a very attractive woman
with a great deal of money to spend. A manufacturer
might resist one, but not the other.'

Despite her blush, Kate laughed goodnaturedly. 'I'm
not sure whether to take that as an insult or a compliment!'

'Merely an observation of life in general and this
business in particular.' He came away from the window
and settled himself in a chair. 'How has Molly been
treating you?'

'Despite my inadequacies, in a very civilised manner.'

He looked suitably impressed. 'Consider yourself
most privileged. In her pursuit of perfection she's been
known to hurl fire and brimstone at professional
incompetence.'

'You sound as if you speak from personal experience?'

'You might say that . . . what have you learnt from
her so far?'

'Apart from office routine?' Kate reflected a moment,
then began to tick off her fingers: 'How to operate the
coffee machine, how to get a letter typed on Friday
afternoons, how to avoid policy meetings and most
important of all, where she hides the brandy.'

'Brandy?' He raised a quizzical eyebrow.

'For medicinal purposes,' she pointed out reasonably.

'Naturally. And where's that?'

She narrowed her eyes. 'Can you be trusted?'

He raised a hand to his head. 'Scout's honour.'

'Your credentials aren't good enough, that was a
Brownie salute . . .'

He burst out laughing. 'So now you've discovered my
secret!'

'I've discovered very little about you. I take it you're
in the fashion business?' She stared at him thoughtfully,

resting her chin in her hand. 'You don't appear to be selling anything?' He shook his head. 'And you're definitely not a designer.'

'How can you tell?'

'For a start, your hair isn't purple, and you aren't wearing earrings.'

'Do all designers look like *that*?'

Her smile widened. 'Those with taste and intelligence don't bother with the earring.'

Again he laughed out loud and then looked at her with quiet amusement in his dark eyes. 'I've a sneaking suspicion you're enjoying your work?'

'Don't let my boss know, he'd probably cut my salary. In this business they usually want to see blood.'

He leaned back in his chair and folded his arms. 'What's he like, your boss?'

'I wouldn't know.' She laughed ironically. 'In this organisation the Director of Buying doesn't bother himself with *my* daily routine.'

'Do I detect a note of disapproval?'

'We haven't met. He was away when I was appointed and junior buyers like myself don't have direct accessibility to the likes of Mr Jones. I'm getting results and presumably that's all that matters.'

'From where I sit I'd say that was his loss.'

Kate waved a dismissive hand. 'But not mine. As it is, too many of his green memos appear on my desk. Like most bosses he appears to hide behind a pile of paperwork.'

He started to say something, but just then the door of the office opened without warning and Simon Forrest breezed in.

'Good morning,' he smiled, rubbing his hands together. 'Did my tub-thumping have any effect on sales?'

Kate was a little taken aback by the sudden intrusion, but returned his smile.

'Hello. I'm afraid I won't know the full story until

this afternoon when all the computer sheets come through. Hold on . . .' She searched among a pile of papers and produced the relevant file. 'Apparently several stores have already rung in for repeats.'

'Sounds like we're in business.' He reached over and picked up the file. 'You should be flattered, it's not for anyone I'd go to all this trouble.'

Simon Forrest appeared to be oblivious of the man seated in the corner, who now stood up abruptly, his expression grim.

'Those figures are none of your business. Put them back.'

Simon looked up startled and his smile disappeared. 'Chester! I didn't see you over there.'

'Obviously.'

Kate looked from one to the other with a puzzled expression. Chester Jones! The Director of Buying! Her eyes widened as she stared up at him in disbelief. Over the weeks Kate's mental image of her elusive employer had grown so awesome and authoritarian that the appearance of an attractive young man in his early thirties wasn't quite what she had been expecting.

Simon shut the file with a resigned shrug and handed it back. 'No harm was meant. Kate knows I'm to be trusted.'

'Like hell you are. I thought I'd made it clear you weren't to show your face around these offices.'

Simon forced a laugh, but Kate could see that he was nervous. 'I'm surprised you take that attitude,' he said defensively, 'after all the free publicity I've given you.'

Chester Jones' eyes narrowed. 'What publicity? What are you talking about?'

'An editorial in the *Sunday Dispatch*. I did a piece on Kate and the new department. And if I do say so myself, it made quite an impression.'

Throughout this hostile exchange, Kate had remained silent, unable to understand what was going on around her, but now, as Chester Jones turned his attention to her, she felt a prickling sensation of apprehension on her own account.

'Is this true?'

'Well, yes,' she replied, her bewilderment at his transformation growing with every second that passed.

'Why didn't you have a word with the Publicity Department before going ahead?'

Kate flinched at his aggressive tone, but her chin went up a fraction. 'I know they usually handle editorials, but it all happened so fast. Next time, I'll . . .'

'There'll be no next time,' he snapped, his eyes blazing. 'Because if you should think of disregarding my warning a second time, Mr Forrest, you'd be well advised to remember that your editor is a good friend of mine.'

Simon raised the flats of his hands in a mock truce. 'Okay, okay! I know when I'm beaten. In future my relationship with Miss Whelan will be purely a personal one . . . I trust you have no objection to us having lunch together?'

Chester Jones made no reply; his manner said it all as he stood, white-faced and angry, and Kate felt her colour deepen when his eyes rested on her with an expression she couldn't fathom. As he steamed out of the office, the door banged behind him.

'But why?' Kate asked Simon later at the restaurant.

'Why does he hate my guts, you mean?' There was a pause as he stirred his coffee. 'You asked me once if I knew Joanna Hill.'

'Yes . . . you said you'd had business dealings.'

'And a lot more besides, until Chester Jones intervened.'

Kate frowned. 'What did he have to do with it?'

Simon's face hardened and he gave a bitter smile.

'*Nothing* goes on in this company he doesn't have anything to do with,' he scowled. 'You'll soon find that out for yourself.'

'But he appeared so friendly at first . . .'

'Naturally. You're young, you're pretty, and you're probably making a great deal of money for him, but if you should ever dare to question his authority the man can be ruthless.'

Kate had no reason to doubt Simon's prediction. Having just witnessed another side to the affable young man she had been speaking to that morning, he might well have grounds for thinking as he did.

'What was it he did?'

'Among other things, he threatened to dismiss Joanna unless she stopped seeing me. She wouldn't, and the rest you can guess.'

Kate sighed and shook her head. 'It doesn't make sense . . . a man in his position behaving in such a despicable manner.'

'Men like Chester Jones have no need of reason on their side, just an inflated ego.'

'But if she really loves you it shouldn't make any difference,' said Kate sympathetically.

He thought about it, studying the bottom of his cup. 'I'm not so sure. He's powerful as well as ruthless. What he wants he usually gets, and he doesn't want me having Joanna.'

Kate did not demur. She had suddenly remembered where it was she had seen Mr Jones before. He it was who had spoken to Joanna Hill that evening in the lift, in such caring and familiar tones.

On her return from lunch, Kate heard her telephone ringing even as she got out of the lift.

'Miss Whelan? This is Miss Johnson, Mr Jones' secretary. Can you be ready to present your Paris report to Mr Jones at three o'clock this afternoon?'

Kate gasped. 'Three o'clock! Well, I don't know . . .'

'I'm afraid it has to be this afternoon, he's off to Italy in the morning.'

Kate slowly placed the receiver and wondered why she had bothered to get out of bed that morning. Until today, she had felt calm and confident of her coming presentation to the Director of Buying. But now? All she felt was anger and confusion: angry at having been caught up in what appeared to be a personal feud and bewildered by Chester Jones' opposition to the editorial. This afternoon, at least, she would be able to present herself in a more professional setting; there were a number of innovations she wanted to carry out in her department, and in particular she was pleased with the half dozen samples she had brought back to strengthen her case.

She crossed the room to the mirror that hung on the opposite wall and stared critically at her reflection, shaking her head at what she saw. She would have preferred something a little more businesslike; a well-cuit suit perhaps, with an upswept hairstyle, and now she regretted her hurried choice that morning. A cream jersey dress that on any other day perfectly comple-mented her warm, honey-coloured skin, but today clung a little too explicitly for the occasion; hugging her full breasts and outlining long shapely legs as she moved. Wishing she had been given a little more notice, she made some attempt to improve her appearance by running a comb through her thick hair, but it refused to be tamed and fell wilfully about her shoulders. Deciding the task to be an impossible one, she gathered together the relevant papers and samples and for the remaining half hour read and re-read her report.

When she could delay no longer Kate made her way to the executive offices. A silent lift deposited her at the sixth floor and she walked hesitantly along a wide cor-ridor, through some swing doors and into a marble-clad reception area. She approached the young and very pretty girl behind the front desk. 'Would you tell me where I could find Mr Jones' office?'

'Do you have an appointment?' the girl enquired. At Kate's affirmative she smiled and pointed at a nearby door. 'You'll find his secretary through there.'

The mahogany door bore the words MR C. J. JONES—DIRECTOR OF BUYING. She stood for a moment, her hand on the latch, then taking a deep breath she went in. Miss Johnson smiled warmly at Kate and looked at her wristwatch. 'Would you like to take a seat and I'll tell Mr Jones you're here.'

She entered the inner office and Kate heard her address an unseen presence. 'Miss Whelan has arrived for her three o'clock appointment, Mr Jones.'

A curt voice answered. 'Would you send her in, please.'

Miss Johnson returned and motioned the young girl to enter. Resisting a primitive urge to turn and run, Kate pushed her hair back with one hand and went in. The door closed softly behind her.

CHAPTER THREE

AFTER the palatial splendour of the reception area, the office was unexpectedly cool and functional and without the usual executive trimmings. There were the essentials: esoteric wall charts, several telephones, official-looking documents awaiting a signature, but one large mahogany desk and several deep armchairs were the only tangible signs of directorial status. Mr Jones, Director of Buying, apparently felt little need to boost his ego, thought Kate apprehensively.

He was standing at his desk studying a plan and as he leant forward a strand of dark brown hair was hanging down over his tanned face. Kate saw now that his boyish looks had been merely an illusion, for looking at his face more closely there was no doubting the experience and strength of his determined chin and wide-set mouth. After a while he raised his head and she blushed as she became conscious of his prolonged gaze upon her, and she silently bemoaned the clinging dress.

To her surprise he gave no sign of recognition, but simply motioned for her to sit down. 'I believe you have a report for me?' he said, his attitude brisk and businesslike.

She handed him her report and sketches and as he sat studying the papers the late afternoon sunlight fell across his face. Was this man, with his piercing, cold eyes and permanent scowl, the same man she had thought so friendly and courteous the first time they met? For a long time he said nothing and she waited anxiously as he slipped one sheet behind another. He looked at them all, then raised his head and nodded towards the samples over her arm.

'Are those from Paris?'

Kate passed him the garments and he studied each at arm's length. After several minutes he laid them aside and slowly sat back in his seat. He nodded towards the report.

'Interesting, but impracticable.'

Surprised and hurt at this casual dismissal of her hard work, Kate let a moment pass, then asked why.

'Profit—or rather its lack. The type of promotion you suggest would involve too much risk and at a time of recession we should stick to what we do best. Innovation is fraught with too many dangers.'

'But with all due respect, we can't afford not to experiment. Younger, more enterprising stores are tempting our customers away.'

His lips compressed. 'You may not be aware, young lady, that we have shareholders to consider. Bennett's strength—and ultimately its profit—has always been to trade in terms of the man in the street.'

'I don't notice his daughter beating a path to our door,' retorted Kate facetiously. She leant forward, her fear of him forgotten in her anger. 'Isn't it time we brushed the cobwebs away, aroused customer interest? How else can we maintain an adequate profit at a time of rising unemployment and general recession?'

She had no chance to continue, for he angrily cut in on her. 'Aren't you forgetting yourself?' he asked coldly. 'I'm not in the habit of being taught my business by junior buyers.'

She blushed. 'I'm sorry. I didn't intend it as rudeness.'

'Possibly,' he said, without conviction. He picked up her report. 'Considering you're a protégé of Miss Cunningham's I'm somewhat surprised at the commercial naïveté. A buyer's main responsibility is to ensure that the right product is selling at the right price, at the right time.' Kate caught her breath as he then proceeded to verbally tear her report to pieces. 'You describe in detail the merchandise displayed in shops and windows, the accessories and themes promoted in the stores. Nowhere do you mention what the Frenchwomen are *buying*. You speak of the colours being promoted, not of the colours being *worn*. As a professional, Miss Whelan, you should know the difference. Are the items on show being *sold*, being *worn*?' He slipped through the pages. 'Your conclusions are based on assumptions rather than hard facts. To suggest we abandon our traditional trade on such flimsy evidence is absurd.' He threw the report on to his desk. 'On this trip you appear to have used your eyes and not your head.' He picked up two samples. 'The fabric and detailing in these would cost an English secretary a month's salary! Who did you have in mind for such merchandise?'

'If given the choice, I believe a lot of women would prefer to have beautifully made clothes . . .'

He cut her off with a decisive move of his arm. 'Of course most women would. But who do you suggest will foot the bill? Her poor overworked husband, already burdened by inflation and higher mortgage commitments?' He gave a sardonic smile. 'Or does she simply charge it to her latest paramour? Do your homework, Miss Whelan—we're being forced to slash prices to win customers, not to raise them!'

'Given the right publicity, I'm certain there's a market for quality merchandise. My editorial with Simon Forrest proves . . .'

'Forrest?' He glanced at her sharply, with sudden speculation. 'Ah, yes . . . Forrest.' The tone in which he pronounced the name left an indelible mark in Kate's mind. 'I wondered when we'd get round to him.' He reached across his desk and picked up a newspaper cutting, and began to read aloud. 'Kate Whelan, a young and attractive buyer, with an instinct for doing the right thing at the right time ... Bennett's gave her opportunity and encouragement, in return she has given them youthful vision and originality.' He threw the cutting back on to the desk. 'What did Simon Forrest get in return, I wonder?' He spoke quietly, his voice bitter. 'Don't let the first mention of your name in print go to your head, Miss Whelan. In fact, I suggest you abandon your quest for individual glory and concentrate on the job in hand. Discover a few home truths about Bennett's average customer, for a start.'

Kate stared at him open-mouthed, stunned by this personal attack, then something inside her baulked.

'What would you know of the average customer? How often do you appear on the sales floor? Talk, listen to what the sales staff have to say, of the customers they have to turn away.'

He leant forward belligerently, his fists closing on the desk before him. 'My experience is based upon ...'

'Memos, reports and last week's figures! What would you know of real people in your paper world.'

'It's a truth you may find unpleasant, Miss Whelan, but in business figures are more reliable than people's opinions. Take your own case, for instance ... without figures to back you up your opinions count for very little.'

She drew in her breath sharply. 'Where's the sense, then, in promoting young buyers when their opinions and suggestions are considered of no consequence?'

'My own thoughts precisely. Perhaps we were a little presumptuous in placing so much responsibility on such young shoulders. Doubtless your youth and spirit would fit a little easier elsewhere.' He handed back her report. 'I suggest you have a word with the personnel manager on your way out.' Kate looked at him for a moment in stricken silence, her face burning, then she turned quickly and walked towards the door. 'Might I also suggest that any further dealings with Simon Forrest be strictly outside office hours? I don't encourage personal relationships within the business.'

She knew she should say nothing and leave, but something was pushing her on. 'Apparently Joanna Hill was your exception to that rule?'

In the silence that followed Chester Jones' eyes blazed, and the muscles that tightened round his mouth betrayed his deep anger. For a long moment he looked hard at Kate across the room before she turned abruptly away and slammed the door behind her. She stood motionless, leaning against the door, her hand still on the knob. Her temples were throbbing as she fought back the tears.

Avoiding the lift and the chance of bumping into someone she might know, she descended the stairs hurt and angry. Once in her office, alone, she sat down and pressed her hands against her head. She held on tightly, then let go and stared at the surface of her desk. She felt empty and very tired, and with the minimum of energy she picked up a blank piece of paper and inserted it into her typewriter. She addressed it to the Personnel Manager and mechanically typed several lines requesting a transfer. When the letter was finished she sat looking at the sheet of paper. That Chester Jones had been romantically involved with Joanna Hill and continued to hold a grudge against his erstwhile rival was the only possible explanation for his behaviour this afternoon, thought Kate. As she sat wondering what to do next, Molly's voice spoke quietly from the doorway.

'Kate, you look dreadful! Has something happened?'

There was no possible denial; her pale cheeks were proof enough. When Molly had read the letter Kate handed to her, she took off her glasses and looked at the young girl in stunned amazement. She listened in silence as Kate, close to tears, told her everything that had happened.

'I simply don't understand why he was so angry at

Simon's article. Look at the publicity Bennett's got. Look at my increased sales. How can he oppose free editorials when his Publicity Department pays exorbitant fees for advertising in the same newspaper?'

Molly sighed and sat down at her desk. 'Doubtless from where you're sitting there seemed everything to be gained from such an arrangement.'

'The whole thing just doesn't make sense!'

Molly spoke quietly, choosing her words with care. 'Joanna Hill became personally involved with Simon Forrest—a relationship that indirectly contributed to her losing her job—and not unreasonably Chester Jones disapproves of him and his column. I blame myself for not having warned you.' She smiled. 'It's too easy to be taken in by his charming manner.'

At this last remark the colour rose in Kate's cheeks. 'Really, Molly, I wasn't born yesterday! *I* haven't the slightest intention of becoming personally involved with the man.'

'What you *intended* would be of little account to Forrest. He's a man without scruples.'

'If you ask me, I think it's simply a case of old-fashioned jealousy on Mr Jones' part . . .'

The look that crossed Molly's face made Kate suspect she might be treading on taboo ground and she thought beter of repeating what Simon Forrest had told her, and what she herself had seen and heard take place between Mr Jones and his former employee, Joanna Hill.

Molly handed back the letter. 'Don't you think you're acting too impulsively? Perhaps you misconstrued what he said.'

Kate shook her head. 'There's no mistake. His meaning was explicit.'

'Why don't you at least sleep on it? You're too good a buyer to be dimissed so unceremoniously.'

'You'd have a difficult job convincing Chester Jones of that,' said Kate gloomily. 'His scathing dismissal of my Paris report was hardly based on a secret admiration for my buying skills.'

'You'd be surprised. The more capable he thinks you are, the harder he pushes.'

'His charming way of winkling out the sheep from the goats, I suppose?' Kate said scornfully.

'His critical stance is a way of testing your professional strength; an opportunity for you to defend your case. If you back down . . .' Molly gave a shrug. 'On the other hand, if you stand up and fight you'll earn his respect.'

'I fought back, but all I earned was his abuse and a transfer.'

Kate signed the letter Molly had returned to her, sealed it within an envelope and placed it in her OUT tray. Without bothering to glance in the mirror, she combed her long hair away from her forehead and threw her jacket over her shoulders. Molly watched as she began to assemble all her personal belongings.

'Perhaps if you apologised to him in the morning . . .'

'In the first place I've done nothing to be sorry for, and in the second place I haven't the slightest intention of remaining with an employer who runs his department in the manner of Attila the Hun.'

Molly sighed. 'If you're really determined to leave the department let me have a word with Chris Lloyd. He's reorganising the Publicity Department and wouldn't say no to having you around the office.'

On Monday Kate found herself seated in a cluttered, glass-enclosed office; merchandise hung limply on plastic hangers, glossy blow-ups portraying models in various states of dress decorated the walls, and every available flat surface was covered by a debris of newspaper clippings, periodicals and a surfeit of pink files. A tall man, who gave an air of being totally disorganised, lunged into the room.

'Hello,' he said cordially to Kate as she introduced herself. 'Molly has been telling me very nice things about you.' He rubbed a hand over his straggly blond hair. 'Would you like some coffee?'

'Very much.'

He asked his secretary to arrange it, and after a leisurely session exchanging personal histories, Kate was pleased to accept a position within the department.

'Things aren't so disorganised as they might appear,' he smiled, motioning towards the surrounding turmoil. 'We've just moved offices.'

Impressed by her record with sportswear, Christopher Lloyd made her responsible for separates within his department. 'It's a new position, so you won't be treading on anyone's toes. This is the first season we've divided the merchandise and the general idea is to work alongside the buying departments. You'll find yourself attending the same collections and making the occasional trip abroad.' He smiled wryly. 'I'm afraid we can't offer you a prestigious title. Your job will only be as important as you make it.'

'As a fugitive from Chester Jones' banana republic I'm only too pleased to forgo any privileges.'

'Sorry to disappoint you, but his authority extends to Publicity.' At the look of dismay on her face, he gently raised the flats of his hands. 'Don't worry, there's a limit even to his power.'

'Nobody appears to have told him that,' Kate added scornfully.

On her journey home her thoughts strayed to Chester Jones. She knew now what Simon Forrest had meant when he complained of his involvement throughout the company. As long as she remained with Bennett's there was simply no escaping the omnipresence of Boy Wonder, thought Kate bitterly and she wondered if transferring to another department had been the wisest move. Perhaps it would be less traumatic to leave the organisation altogether. But anger at his unjust accusations and callous behaviour strengthened her resolve to prove her worth on his home territory.

The last few days had been horribly suspenseful, and that evening Kate went home and stretched out on the couch. She kicked off her shoes, laid her head on her arms and slept soundly for two hours. At ten minutes past nine the phone woke her from a deep sleep. She got up from the sofa and felt in the dark for the telephone.

'Kate? Is that you?' It was Molly. 'Are you doing anything special tonight? Could I come over?'

Half an hour later they were sitting together over a pot of black coffee and ham sandwiches.

'How did the meeting with Chris go?' Molly enquired, biting into her third sandwich.

'I'm to start next week. Quite honestly, I'm looking forward to the change of pace.'

'Rubbish! It was a theatrical gesture and you'll be bored stiff within a month.'

'You're probably right,' Kate laughed, and passed Molly a second cup of coffee.

'Then won't you reconsider your decision?' pleaded Molly.

Kate paused and studied her cup. 'The decision isn't really mine, is it? Let's not forget it was Chester Jones who suggested my transfer in the first place—and he's the boss.'

Molly stood up and walked over to the window, drew aside the curtain, then wandered back to her chair.

'I had lunch with Joanna Hill today.' Kate looked up, surprised. 'She was very upset at what happened.'

'Who told her?'

'Chester.'

'But why should it concern . . .?' Her voice trailed away as Molly's answer struck home. 'So I was right all along,' said Kate bitterly, as her bridled anger turned into contempt.

Molly lit a cigarette. 'That's just it, Kate. I'm afraid you weren't.' She drew deeply on her cigarette. 'Joanna Hill is Chester Jones' sister.'

Kate put down her cup and stared at Molly disbelievingly. 'Sister?' she repeated uncomprehendingly.

Molly tapped ash off her cigarette. 'His half-sister, actually. His mother married twice. Both parents are now dead and he's her guardian.'

That explained the familiarity of his features, thought Kate numbly. In fact, it explained a great deal ... She winced inwardly, remembering what she had thought, what she had *said* to him ...

'What a fool I've been,' she murmured, but as her astonishment wore off certain things still did not make sense. 'It doesn't explain his critical attitude towards *me*. I replaced his sister after she'd left. And with his approval, if you remember.'

'It's a long story. Without his knowledge—I believe he was abroad at the time—Joanna applied and was accepted as a trainee buyer with Bennett's. She made no mention of her brother at the interview and only after her letter of acceptance did she tell him.'

'I suppose Personnel failed to make any connection between the different names.'

'It placed him in an awkward situation. Reluctant to jeopardise her career, he decided to keep things quiet— perhaps unwisely.'

'Didn't she consider the damage she might have caused his career?'

Molly smiled. 'You don't know Joanna! Anyhow, things went smoothly enough until Simon Forrest came upon the scene. Chester decided to take me into his confidence and asked me to keep a motherly eye on Joanna.'

'But why be so concerned over a normal boy-girl relationship?'

'Like any other buyer, Joanna was responsible for a great deal of money. Unlike other buyers she was becoming emotionally involved within her profession. Under Simon's influence she began to buy the wrong merchandise—merchandise that refused to sell.'

'I still don't understand. Why should he want Joanna to buy the wrong merchandise?'

'When you've been buying as long as I have, Kate, you get a feeling for people. Chester and I both have a 'feeling' for Simon Forrest.'

'I'm sorry, but I still don't . . .'

'We believe—and this must go no farther—that Simon Forrest is paid by certain manufacturers for those orders he can persuade influential buyers to place with them.'

The pieces began to fall into place.

'So that when Chester saw signs of *my* possible involvement with Simon Forrest, he assumed the worst,' said Kate. 'It explains quite a few things.'

'We've no concrete evidence, but all the signs are there. His excessive life-style, associations with dubious manufacturers, his regular promotion of known losers.'

Kate frowned. 'I'm not totally convinced . . . Look what his editorial did for my sales figures!'

'Oh, in the beginning he plays his cards well. As I said once before, he's a smooth operator.'

Kate blushed; at the back of her mind there still lingered a suspicion that Simon Forrest's engaging personality had perhaps been the decisive factor in her own case.

'Joanna was pretty angry at her brother's treatment of you and intends to apologise on his behalf.'

'She's no reason to, now that I know the full story.'

'I suspect she also wants to check out my story of there being nothing between you and Simon Forrest. Perhaps you could put her mind at ease?'

'You mean that despite what's happened she feels the same about him?'

'Nothing we could say would persuade her against him. Unfortunately, it's caused something of a family feud.'

As reluctant as Kate was to have any further dealings with Chester Jones, memory of Joanna Hill's unhappy face softened her intent. 'Of course I'll see her. Do you have a phone number?'

CHAPTER FOUR

FULL of doubts and misgivings and wishing heartily that she hadn't agreed to see Joanna Hill, Kate found herself ringing the bell of a small basement flat off the King's Road. She hardly recognised the pretty young girl who greeted her at the door as the distressed creature of several weeks past; the dark shadows had gone from her eyes and her freshly scrubbed face left no doubt as to her family connections. She led the way into a room empty of furniture save for several large tea chests, and her warm and friendly manner soon dispelled any apprehension Kate might have felt at making the visit.

'You'll have to excuse the mess, I'm afraid. I only moved in this week and I haven't had much time to organise myself.' Joanna apologised for there being no chairs in the room, disappeared, and returned with a stool for Kate and a large cushion for herself.

'Would you prefer tea or coffee? Although it's only fair to warn you the coffee's a yukky instant version.'

'Then tea it shall be.'

'I didn't really expect to see you,' Joanna called from the kitchen. 'A confrontation with Chester tends to put people off the rest of his family.'

'A confrontation with Chester Jones tends to put people off Chester Jones,' smiled Kate.

'My thoughts precisely,' replied Joanna, carrying in two steaming mugs of tea on a tray. 'He's a case of "*light blue paper and stand well clear*".'

As she sat on the cushion and made room beside her for the tray, Kate noticed her frayed jeans and bare feet. 'Not exactly elegant living, is it?' she smiled, handing Kate a mug. 'You must promise to come back when the flat is finished and I can serve you dinner with all the trimmings—like chairs and a table.'

She leaned back against one of the tea chests and her voice took on a more serious note. 'I was so sorry to hear what happened. It was so unfair of Chester.'

Kate shrugged. 'Perhaps if I hadn't lost my temper things might have been different. If I'd been more rational . . .'

'Oh, there's no need to be tactful because he's my brother. *Because* he's my brother I know his nasty habits.'

Kate smiled as if to say, what's the use of talking, it's happened, and to spare them both any painful reminiscences she steered the conversation in another direction.

'You're looking a lot happier than when we last met.'

Joanna waved her arm around the room. 'I've a new flat. And Chester's away for two whole weeks, which means a fortnight without him nagging me about Simon.'

'It's that bad, is it?' smiled Kate.

'It can be. It's partly the reason I got this flat; to prove my independence.' She sat still, watching her bare toes. 'On a good day he's really quite sweet, if only he would let me live my *own* life and not his version of it.' She looked up at Kate, puzzled. 'Do you know he blamed Simon for my dismissal? He refuses to accept that it was simply *me*—his own sister, bungling the job. A family failure!'

'I don't think that's entirely fair,' said Kate gently.

'Don't attempt to defend him after the unfair treatment he handed out to you! If it wasn't for his blind prejudice towards Simon you'd still be a buyer.' More quietly Joanna added: 'And so might I.'

'Do you still miss the rag trade?' asked Kate.

'Not any more!' Joanna spoke with a passionate certainty. 'In a way Chester did me a good turn—did us both a good turn. My dream of a glamorous fashion career hadn't taken into account the hard grind it involved. Besides, I made a mistake and he had no choice. To make me the exception would have led to questions being asked and perhaps placing his own job in jeopardy.' She smiled and drew her knees up under her chin. 'We both couldn't afford to be out of work.'

'I suppose morally you're his dependant?'

She nodded. 'That's the pity of it all. I know that despite everything, his sole concern is for my happiness.' She sat quietly and related their family history.

Chester's father had been something of an adventurer. Born of Czech parents who had settled in England, he travelled extensively; a troubleshooter who resolved the technical problems that regularly occurred on oil drilling sites. At a time when the growth of the oil industry far outstripped the expertise then available, his experience as an engineer was much in demand, and the financial inducements were large. On such a trip in the Middle East, he met and married Chester's mother, a Scottish nurse. It was a happy marriage; they travelled the world together with their small son, enjoying a life of chauffeur-driven cars, luxurious hotels and first class travel. Only on her husband's death did his wife discover that their wealth had been only apparent; their high living subsidised not by capital, but by exorbitant expenses, gratefully paid by prosperous clients. In reality, outgoings had equalled income and no provision had been made for mother and son. Struggling to support them both, she eventually managed to build up a small successful business, buying and selling antiques, and several years later she met Joanna's father, a loving husband, but something of a drain on her business profits. They both died in a car crash ten years ago and Chester, still in his early twenties, took on the responsibility of a twelve-year-old girl and set up home for them both.

Joanna traced patterns on the bare floorboards.

'Mother's problems were caused by two irresponsible husbands and I think Chester wants to save me from a similar fate . . .'

'Is that so terrible?'

She shrugged. 'Not as terrible as the future being set up for *him* by Erika Gibbs.'

'Erika Gibbs?' The name rang a bell.

Joanna wrinkled her nose in distaste. 'A painted doll who works on the *Evening Gazette* and feeds Chester malicious gossip about Simon.' Her voice hardened. 'She's resented Simon ever since he got the job she was after, with the *Sunday Dispatch*. Without her influence I think I might have talked Chester around.'

'What is her influence?' asked Kate.

'That of a calculating miss who makes herself available and amiable to Chester. She's that determined to hook him.'

'What does your brother think about it?'

'He doesn't. His hysterical concern for me and Simon makes him incapable of judgment. He's the one who needs looking after, not me.'

'Why has he never married?' asked Kate, her curiosity stirred.

'Because he considers being responsible for one female is headache enough without adding a second. If you ask me, he simply uses it as an excuse to dangle in front of girl-friends with something more than a light flirtation on their mind.'

'Well, at least you'll be able to prove your independence with your new flat, and then there's your job at the airport. How's it going, by the way? Still interpreting for lots of dishy Frenchmen?'

Joanna's cheeks flushed with irritation. 'Don't you understand? I'm not interested in other men, French or otherwise. Why is it no one takes Simon and me seriously?'

'Chester appears to.'

'On the contrary. It's because he doesn't believe Simon's serious intentions that he's against him.'

'You mean only marriage would convince him?'

'I told you—he's incapable of judgment. One moment he's questioning Simon's *honourable intentions* and the next he explodes at the very mention of marriage.'

'Why don't you call his bluff?' suggested Kate. 'You're of an age to marry without his consent. And seeing you happily married might change his mind about Simon.'

'No ... It's not as simple as that. Simon wants to establish his career, to be financially secure before taking on family commitments.'

'Is that what *you* want?'

The floor occupied the girl's attention. 'What I want is marriage and a family, but just now what Simon says seems to make more sense ...'

'And *your* feelings are of no consequence? It seems to me that Simon and your brother have more in common than you suppose.'

'You're right, of course. It's something I've hardly dared admit to myself and, to be honest, I'm more than a little tired of playing piggy in the middle to two grown men.'

'Speaking as one who knows,' observed Kate, 'brothers who zealously guard their sisters' honour may sound romantic, but can be something of a pain in the neck.'

Joanna giggled. 'If I agreed to Chester's terms, he'd have me set up in a suburban semi with double glazing and wall-to-wall boredom, Sunday supplement style.'

'It's a life that makes a lot of people happy.'

'Not me, nor Chester. If the truth were known, he's spent all his life fighting against just that, middle class mediocrity.'

'You surprise me. Chester Jones, dependable head of the buying department, is not my idea of the traditional rebel!' said Kate.

'Don't you believe it. Despite appearances my brother remains very much his father's son. In another age he would have sailed the seven seas seeking adventure, now he just goes on lots of buying trips to compensate. It's his wandering spirit that eludes all those conniving females.' Joanna smiled wryly. 'And the one person he doesn't want me to marry is someone like himself.'

Interrupted by the telephone ringing, Joanna reached behind one of the tea chests and picked up the receiver. 'Darling! I didn't expect you back till tomorrow.' She mouthed an aside. 'It's Simon.' She crossed her legs pow-wow fashion. 'Guess who's here? Kate Whelan.' She placed her hand over the mouthpiece. 'He sends his love.'

As curious as Kate had once been about her employer, each new revelation by his sister had left her feeling distinctly uncomfortable. Unwittingly she had intruded into his personal life and her guilt, aggravated by the tedium and discomfort of a long bus journey home, determined Kate to avoid any further communication with his sister. Why should she increase her chances of running into Chester Jones again; one confrontation with him had been sufficient. In their domestic dilemma both brother and sister appeared determined to have their own way, and Kate had no intention of taking up with either of the opposing factions.

Joanna had other ideas; at lunchtime the following day she presented herself in Kate's office. 'Simon had to cancel our lunch date and as I was in your vicinity and it happens to be my birthday, I wondered if you'd help me celebrate. My treat, of course.'

Not wanting to appear ungracious, Kate accepted the invitation.

Lunch was a relaxed cheerful affair, full of inconsequential girlish chatter. Joanna was in high spirits and entertained Kate with stories of her new job, of the odd propositions she had received from several passengers as well as the strange requests from some of the more nervous travellers. The laughter of the two girls brought forth indulgent smiles from other diners, while their obvious physical attractions drew looks of admiration from the men present. Not until they were preparing to leave did Joanna become serious.

'Simon was very upset at your dismissal,' she told Kate.

'Transfer. There is a difference.'

'An academic one. Chester left you no alternative.'

Irritated, but not surprised that Joanna had discussed the matter with Simon Forrest, Kate spoke firmly. 'I appreciate your concern, but I'd rather you didn't discuss my affairs with Simon.'

There was a moment of awkward silence.

'He mentioned calling Chester ... to explain matters.'

Kate flushed with suppressed anger. With Simon Forrest pleading her cause she might as well hand in her notice now!

'His interference would do more harm than good. Your brother believed we were personally involved, and a phone call on my behalf would only strengthen that suspicion ...' She stopped as she saw Joanna's look of concern. 'Naturally, such a thing was pure fantasy on your brother's part, but it was hopeless trying to explain that to him.'

At Kate's hasty denial, Joanna's worried face relaxed into a smile and they parted good friends. Strange, thought Kate, walking back to the office, how the same facial features of brother and sister could create two distinct impressions; one sensitive and vulnerable, the other strong and determined. Kate had found the girl refreshing company and regretted they had not met in other circumstances, but Joanna's charming manner had yet to blur Kate's memory of her brother's despicable behaviour.

What did cause oblivion was being thrown headlong into her new job. After months of being understaffed, Christopher had presented Kate on her first day with a backlog of laborious tasks, and daily the list seemed to swell: innumerable visits to the branches, assessing customer reaction and attitudes to advertisements, analysis of sales and advertising costs, consumer research processed and passed on. Attention to such trivia, Christopher insisted, was the only way of grasping how publicity operated at grass roots. Certainly it was the toughest.

After several weeks of detailed clerical work Christopher invited Kate along to a mid-season publicity party. Colliers, a successful sports company, were promoting a new line in leisure wear and an elegant buffet, with a generous supply of pleasant wine, held promise of an enjoyable evening. Kate was pleased to see so many familiar faces, but groaned inwardly when she saw Simon Forrest coming towards her. He excused himself to Kate's companions and steered her by the elbow to a quiet corner. She resented the familiarity he publicly displayed towards her and coolly declined his offer of another drink.

'I understand you and Chester Jones crossed paths?' he said, eyeing her over the rim of his glass.

'Crossed swords is more like it!'

'You should have called me. I do have *some* influence in the fashion trade.'

'After being given my marching orders I'm too much of a realist to believe another buyership would be that easy to come by . . .'

'Nonsense. You're in possession of two very negotiable assets: youth and vision. You could have taken your pick.'

'I'm flattered that you should think so, but you forget I would need a reference from Chester Jones, and I'd hardly expect a glowing report from that direction.'

'Not everyone treats his word as gospel, and if you're interested I can still pull some strings for my friends.'

'Thank you, but no,' said Kate firmly. 'Please, let's drop the subject.'

Despite the ill-will she still bore her former employer, Kate resisted the temptation to place her trust or future with Simon Forrest. Although not convinced of his villainy, she had yet to be persuaded of the man's integrity.

He shrugged his shoulders and smiled. 'I must say you're looking very well. I trust the new job suits you and that Christopher is looking after you?'

'Yes on both accounts, although things were a trifle confusing at first.'

'It won't take you long to make your mark, and then I'll expect you to throw lots of business my way, remember . . .'

Kate pointedly ignored this last remark and enquired about his recent trip. 'Joanna tells me you've been away.'

'I went to see what our cousins were up to on Seventh Avenue.'

'Sounds intriguing.'

Simon Forrest possessed that most envied of all nature's gifts; the ability to tell a funny story, and his trip abroad had supplied him with plenty of raw material. His conversation was peppered with humorous anecdotes and as she listened, for the first time Kate understood a little of his appeal to Joanna. Here was an aimable, good-looking man who appeared to delight in female company; easy to see the hold he might exert over a younger, more impressionable woman, thought Kate.

But what might appeal to the opposite sex, and to Joanna in particular, apparently found little sympathy with her brother, whose dark Slavic humours doubtless looked with suspicion upon such genteel refinements, thought Kate sardonically. Just imagine having to live alongside those black moods; small wonder that Joanna moved in the opposite direction! And yet according to her women beat a path to his door. As a buyer, Kate knew there was no accounting for some people's taste.

In mid-conversation, Simon put an arm around her shoulders and led her towards two empty seats. On the way a photographer stepped across their path.

'Would you mind letting me have a picture for my magazine?'

Pausing a moment to oblige the young man and identify themselves, Simon continued. 'I seem to be doing all the talking. How about you? Joanna tells me you and she have become friends.'

Kate smiled. 'We had lunch together. She's delightful company.'

He nodded agreement. 'Amazingly so, considering her lineage.'

'Chester, you mean?'

'He's a type I'd long supposed extinct.' He raised his eyes to the ceiling. 'Just imagine having him for a brother!'

'Or a brother-in-law, perhaps?'

He shook his head. 'There's no way he'd ever give his approval to our marriage.'

'Why should you need it?'

'Because it would break Joanna's heart if it were otherwise.'

Concern for her brother's approval was hardly the image Joanna had presented the other evening, thought Kate cynically.

'I would have thought sibling jealousy was as traditional as rice at weddings. I'm surprised you let it bother you.'

He studied his drink. 'Marriage might appear attrac-

tive to Joanna simply *because* of family opposition.
Given Chester's approval she might think otherwise.'

'I think John Wayne had the answer to your problem,'
Kate told him.

'John Wayne?'

'He simply threw the woman over his saddle and rode
off into a distant sunset.'

Simon threw back his head and laughed. 'I'll give it
plenty of thought.'

He leaned over to put out his cigarette and his voice
took on a serious tone. 'Joanna's been through a traumatic year; losing her job, leaving home, Chester's opposition to our relationship, and now with her new job
and flat ... She needs to be given breathing space.
Marriage isn't the refuge she supposes it to be and at
the present moment it would be a mistake for us to
make any hasty decision. Joanna is still a young girl.
She must be sure.'

'She's not so much younger than me,' Kate pointed
out.

He smiled indulgently. 'Some people are wise at birth,
others take a little longer. You must remember that
Joanna was educated at a convent until she was eigh-
teen, from whence she remained at home under her
brother's watchful eye.'

'What about girl friends?'

'Most of them are away at college or abroad ...
Perhaps that's why she values your friendship so much.'

A frantic wave from Christopher, signalling her to
join him and several companions, prevented further
conversation, and as she left Simon with a promise to
ring Joanna soon, Kate immediately regretted the commitment and the further involvement it might mean.
Unwittingly she was becoming more and more entangled
in their emotional web.

Waking on Saturday morning to warm sunshine

streaming through the windows, Kate dressed cheerfully
for her usual weekend trip to the local market. After a
week of decisions and dilemmas, she looked forward to
wandering aimlessly about the stalls with their mouthwatering displays of fruit and vegetables and enjoying
the friendly banter of the stallholders. Struggling with
several bags of weekend shopping, she bumped into
Molly, whose sister lived nearby.

'You've saved me a phone call,' smiled Molly, reliev-
ing Kate of one of her parcels. 'I was going to ask you to
come to lunch, but we can have a late breakfast instead.'

In a local teashop, warm and muggy with a delicious
smell of baking, the two friends exchanged news over
fresh orange juice and hot croissants.

'I've been asked to pass on messages of regrets from
several young men who've enquired after you at the
office,' Molly told her.

Kate grinned. 'To be truthful, I've been too busy to
feel homesick myself. I've been travelling all over the
West Country and Paddington Station has practically
become a home from home. Fortunately things are
looking up. Christopher treated me to a social outing
last week.'

'Fraternisation in office hours! Tut, tut! What would
Chester Jones have to say about that?' Molly mockingly
admonished.

Kate waved a dismissive hand. 'Nothing so sinful,'
she laughed, and went on to relate her evening to Molly,
whose smile faded at the mention of Simon Forrest.

'That man has never been known to turn down an
invitation.'

'Be fair—after all, his column is pretty influential and
he would say he was only doing his job. You and
Chester can't simply wish him away.'

'Perhaps we could stick pins in a waxen image.'

'Doesn't Joanna credit Chester with doing precisely
that already?'

'With Joanna everything is a little larger than life. She has an extraordinary lively imagination.' Molly paused, then said tentatively: 'It's funny, but in some ways you and she are very similar. Both of you have lost your job over Simon Forrest, but despite the flashing signs and warning bells you both dig in your heels over the man and cast Chester in the villain's role. I suppose with so much in common, friendship was bound to ensue. How is she, by the way? Still flying her flag of independence?'

'Ruthlessly. Decorating the new flat, her new job . . .'

'World's best therapy for getting a man out of your system.'

'I don't know if she wants to get him "out of her system". Depends on which man you had in mind.'

Molly shrugged. 'Fortunately that's Joanna's decision. Problems concerning the opposite sex I've long left behind.'

'Who are you kidding?' smiled Kate, mindful of a recent passion in Molly's life.

'Oh, the men are still there, but experience has taught me how not to let them become a problem. After all, there has to be some compensation for growing older . . .' grinned Molly, draining the juice from her glass, then saying thoughtfully as she replaced it on the table:

'I suppose you think it none of my business, Kate, but is it wise to see quite so much of Joanna?'

'Wise?' queried Kate.

'Perhaps that's the wrong word . . . It's simply that I'd hate to see you caught a second time in Chester's line of fire.'

'So would I,' grimaced Kate, 'but against my better judgment I seem to have been caught up in their affair.'

'Don't let Joanna use you as an emotional dustbin. You've your own life to lead, remember.'

'Does Chester know about her new flat?' Kate asked.

Molly frowned. 'I don't know, but if he doesn't,' she raised her eyes to the ceiling, 'I don't look forward to his homecoming when he finds the bird has flown.'

'I'm sure it will be the best for both of them.'

'I'm sure you're right,' agreed Molly.

After several cups of dawdled coffee, they paid the bill and emerged from the café into brilliant sunshine, and at Molly's suggestion they unloaded Kate's shopping and spent the rest of the day browsing round the antique stalls.

On Sunday morning, the sharp ringing of the telephone intruded upon Kate's leisurely breakfast. It was Joanna inviting her to dinner on Monday evening.

'It's a little short notice, I'm not sure if . . .'

She wasn't allowed to finish. 'I've just completed the dining room and I desperately want to show it off. Please say you'll come!'

Moved by the other girl's genuine excitement and feeling guilty about not having called her, Kate felt unable to refuse the invitation. She put down the receiver slowly and sighed at her lack of resolve. Hadn't Molly once taught her the diplomatic way of saying no, and hadn't she practised daily with hardbitten businessmen? Why then was she unable to retire gracefully from this continuing charade?

CHAPTER FIVE

KATE was unprepared for the transformation of the basement flat since her last visit, and as Joanna flung open the door of the sitting room she giggled with pleasure at Kate's look of surprise. Soft printed fabrics covered chairs and sofa and framed windows, a collection of bric-à-brac filled the shelves, small bowls of fresh flowers were casually arranged about the room, while cushions and lighted candles created a gentle, relaxed atmosphere.

'You did all this?' Kate marvelled.

'Juggling cloth samples and colour charts is something I've always enjoyed doing, and with a new flat I've been able to indulge myself to excess.'

'Success, more likely.' Kate settled herself on to a pile of cushions and gratefully accepted a glass of sherry. 'Something smells good?'

'As promised, I've prepared you an elaborate meal with all the trimmings; smoked trout followed by filet mignon followed by crême brulée. And as a special treat . . .' She held up a bottle of St Emilion.

'All this gracious living on my behalf makes me feel a little guilty,' said Kate.

'As a matter of fact . . .' Joanna began to occupy herself with a vase of flowers, 'Simon will be joining us for dinner. I thought I mentioned it to you . . .' She gave Kate a little glance. 'I hope you don't mind?'

No, she had not mentioned it, and yes, she did mind. Kate's good humour gave way to anger at the manner in which she had been used and at Joanna's deliberate deception; her own feelings apparently of no consequence.

Conscious of Kate's silence, Joanna swung round and spoke breathlessly. 'Simon and I have decided to marry and I wanted you to be the first to know our secret!' She gave a nervous smile; uncertain of the response to her news. 'Tonight was to be a small celebration.'

Hardly a second elapsed before Kate raised her glass. 'Congratulations. That's wonderful news.'

'We think so. I only hope Chester does.'

'He doesn't know yet?' Joanna shook her head. 'Shouldn't you tell him before it becomes public knowledge?'

Joanna settled herself in one of the easy chairs. 'Apart from telling you, we're keeping the engagement secret for the moment.' Kate hazarded a silent guess as to whose decision that might have been. 'When the time is right,' Joanna continued, 'I shall tell him.'

Would there ever be a time convenient enough, thought Kate, for Joanna to tell her brother of her engagement to Simon Forrest?

'You haven't shown me your ring,' smiled Kate.

Joanna shifted in her chair and held out her left hand. 'Would you believe, we decided things so quickly Simon hasn't even had time to buy me one.' She rubbed her bare finger ruefully. 'I suppose it will make it easier keeping our secret . . .'

'When are you planning to get married?'

Joanna smiled wryly. 'We haven't thought that far ahead, but when we do decide, we shall quietly go off somewhere and have a simple ceremony.'

'Thank goodness for that,' Kate teased. 'For one ghastly moment I thought you were going to ask me to be chief bridesmaid!'

Though somewhat sceptical of the vagueness of the arrangements, nevertheless Kate was happier to remain in ignorance of Joanna's affairs than to be one of the principal players.

Joanna kicked off her shoes and tucked her feet up

beneath her. 'I can't tell you how happy I am, Kate. Don't you envy me my good fortune?'

Kate nodded and smiled. 'Your good fortune and your romantic nature.'

'I've a sneaking suspicion you're being cynical and this evening that simply isn't allowed. Speaking of good fortune, I almost forgot ... I've just received some good news, an unexpected legacy from my grandmother who died last year. Nothing grand, but enough to make me less of a financial burden on Chester. Of course, it will take a few months to sort out the legal wrangles.'

'How wonderful for you! I'm so pleased everything has turned out well.'

'So, you see, this evening is something of a double celebration,' said Joanna. 'Let me fill your glass.'

As she stood up to replenish their drinks, the door bell rang and she frowned at her watch. 'That must be Simon, earlier than he expected. Would you excuse me?'

Left alone in the room, Kate sat motionless for some few moments, her empty glass still in her hands. As she recalled her recent conversation with Simon Forrest and his forthright views on the state of matrimony, Joanna's sudden announcement had come as something of a surprise ... Explaining his caution the other evening, Simon appeared to have prudence and cool reason on his side so that now Kate was at a loss to understand this recent turn of events. Had his denial of marriage plans been merely a ploy on his part, to remove any suspicion she might have had as to his true intent? Or did Joanna's surprise legacy have anything to do with his more recent decision? She sighed inwardly at her uncharitable thoughts, then stood up and wandered over to a small bookcase.

'Darling, what a lovely surprise! When did you get back?'

'This morning. I thought I'd call in to see how you were getting along.'

The voice that floated in from the hall froze Kate to the spot. It was the moment she had been dreading, and she felt the colour drain from her face as she turned to face her former employer. Engaged in a humorous exchange with his sister, their arms linked, Chester Jones broke off in mid-sentence when he realised they were not alone. There was a pause, a tremor of curiosity in his eyes.

'I'm sorry . . . I didn't know you had company.'

'Don't be formal. Kate's not *company*—she's a good friend. Have you time for a drink?'

With her heart hammering Kate retreated to a corner seat. Only when she set down her empty glass did she notice her hand trembling, and she wondered why this man's presence should arouse such confusion within her—he was after all her *ex*-employer. He was also, she admitted grudgingly, very good-looking, and as he wandered idly about looking at things, the spacious room appeared less so; his tall frame unsuited to the small floral prints and china ornaments. Acutely conscious of her own unease as she was, his relaxed manner and apparent disregard of *her* presence irritated Kate beyond measure.

'You appear to have settled comfortably into the flat. How's the new job?'

His sister grimaced. 'Madly unexciting.'

He shook his head as if she were a little mad. 'Excitement isn't usually to be found in the terms of reference, it's what you make of the job yourself. Besides, you've only been there several weeks.'

'I've a low threshold of pain,' laughed Joanna.

'I would have thought the job suited you perfectly; travellers in the night, distant horizons, etcetera, etcetera.'

She grunted. 'Flight delays and lost baggage hardly add up to much gaiety about the place.'

'Do you think you've given it a fair chance? Things worthwhile usually take time.'

'I suppose I simply don't have that time to spare.'

'You ought to make the effort, Jo. Good jobs aren't so easy to find.'

'Tell that to Kate.'

Kate silently cursed Joanna as Chester Jones looked casually in her direction and shrugged his shoulders. 'For someone with youth and ability, as one door closes another usually opens.'

'It depends on who's doing the closing, and how hard,' was Joanna's cryptic response.

'From what I hear Publicity is benefiting enormously from Miss Whelan's presence.'

'But is Miss Whelan?'

His face wore an expression of quizzical amusement as he looked at Kate and repeated his sister's question. '*Is* Miss Whelan?'

Kate felt her cheeks redden as she made an attempt to appear likewise amused. 'I believe it's a defendant's privilege to remain silent.'

'But hardly a female trait. I suggest you coach Joanna in the art.'

At this remark Joanna loudly protested and playfully threw a well aimed cushion at his head. Kate was a little bemused by the warm and easy relationship that appeared to exist between brother and sister; not at all what she had been led to expect.

'Speaking of art, I almost forgot . . .' Chester went out to the hall and returned with a brown, flat parcel. 'A belated birthday gift. I bought them in Italy on my last trip.'

Joanna unwrapped a family of three small delicate watercolours.

'Oh, Chester, they're perfect!' She kissed him impulsively. 'How generous you are!' She placed each of them upon the mantelshelf, then stepped back, her head on one side, to survey the effect. 'Absolutely perfect!'

'I'm pleased they meet with your approval.'

'That's something I do miss,' said Joanna, 'all those overseas buying trips: perfumes from Paris, silks from Italy . . .'

'And tulips from Amsterdam,' smiled Chester wryly. 'A romantic's view of a cut-throat business.' He suddenly looked at his watch and got to his feet. 'I must go. I only looked in to give you your present and see if there was anything you needed.'

'Are you sure you won't stay for supper?'

'I'm already dining out this evening.'

Her tone hardened. 'With Erika, I suppose. Watch out she doesn't grind your bones to make her bread.'

'She's vegetarian, actually. She leaves the blood sports to you.' As Joanna accompanied him to the door he nodded goodbye to Kate, who could not help smiling at the smooth practised manner in which he had handled his sister's verbal thrust. When Joanna returned, she curled up opposite in an armchair and rolled her eyes. 'Thank goodness Simon is never punctual. I simply couldn't have coped with a war of the worlds this early in the evening!'

Kate smiled. 'Doubtless both of them would have behaved like English gentlemen.'

Joanna cupped her chin in her hand and grimaced. 'Simon's Irish, and I suppose you could say Chester was only English by default, so neither would be obliged to be gentlemen.'

'I think you're being unduly pessimistic. Your brother appeared very affable this evening. In fact, seeing you both together, no one would ever suspect you of having anything other than a loving brother-and-sister relationship.'

Joanna pursed her lips and studied the carpet. 'We appear to have reached an unspoken agreement; he won't mention Simon if I don't mention Erika.'

'That didn't appear to be the case this evening,' commented Kate.

'Mm ... I'm afraid I'm less honourable than my brother, but then he has age and wisdom on his side.'

Thirty minutes later Simon arrived, and after her earlier traumatic experience, Kate slipped easily into a passive role, pleased to be entertained by the happy couple for the remainder of the evening.

Kate spent the following week happily immersed in a new publicity campaign. Impressed by her ability to get things done—a precious talent in a business with its fair share of talkers—Christopher had allowed her to spread her wings a little, and, in conjunction with the International Wool Secretariat and other similar worthy bodies, she was to prepare an autumn promotion on natural fibres. Advertisements had to be placed in the national press and TV, air time booked on local radio, window displays planned, leaflets printed and distributed.

Late one evening Kate was finalising the budget figures when the door from the main office opened and a girl poked her head in.

'Is Mr Lloyd still here?'

'He left over two hours ago.'

The girl bit her bottom lip and held up a file of papers. 'I was supposed to give him this at lunchtime, but I fell behind with my typing. It's for the branch managers' conference tomorrow morning.'

'Can't it wait until then?'

'The meeting starts at nine o'clock sharp and these figures are wanted beforehand. Mr Lloyd is one of the speakers and offered to hand them in. My boss will kill me if they don't get them!'

Kate took the papers and read a label pinned to the front. 'Cumberland Terrace—it's on my way home. I'll drop it in this evening.'

A look of relief flooded the girl's face. 'Thanks ever

so much. I'd go myself, only I've got a special date . . .'
The grateful messenger smiled cheerio from the doorway
and disappeared from sight.

An hour later Kate located the address on the file—
an elegant Regency building overlooking Regent's Park,
and as she entered the large imposing entrance hall, an
elderly porter emerged from a rear office. She explained
her errand and he languidly operated a small switchboard.

'There's a package for you at reception, sir.
Apparently it's urgent. Would you like it sent up?' He
waited as the man at the other end spoke, then looked
over towards Kate with his eyebrows raised. 'I understand it's from your office. . . . Yes, sir . . . Very well,
I'll send it up.' He pulled out the plug and jerked his
head in the general direction of the stairs. 'Mr Jones
says you're to go on up.'

Mr Jones says you're to go on up. Mr Jones? Kate
felt the breath leave her body at the dreadful realisation
of where she was. There had been no name on the label
and she had rashly assumed the address to be a business
one, certainly not the private residence of Chester Jones.
She tentatively suggested leaving the file at reception,
but the porter, the task completed to *his* satisfaction,
had already retreated with his newspaper to the small
gas fire in his office and was otherwise engaged in more
worldly matters.

Seeing no alternative, she moved reluctantly across
the large square hall and slowly climbed the curving
staircase, her long, elegant legs momentarily distracting
the porter's attention. She reached the first floor and
frowned as she caught sight of her windblown reflection
in a long mirror, further convinced that her presence in
such austere surroundings was a terrible mistake. But in
spite of its unprovoked attack on her long, loose hair,
the cold wind had compensated its victim with glowing
cheeks and shining eyes, and she drew a sidelong glance

of admiration from a gentleman passing her on the stairs.

Apprehensive at her reception and feeling warm from the climb, she undid the buttons of her wool jacket, unconscious of her silk shirt clinging to her damp skin and outlining firm, full breasts. When she reached flat number five she took a deep breath and rang the bell. She would be brief but polite. A familiar voice called out: 'Come in.'

She hesitated, then stepped through the partly open door and into a small lobby. The voice came again. 'I'm in the shower, George.'

Resisting the invitation and wondering who George might be, Kate decided to remain within sight of the front door. Receiving no acknowledgment, the figure of Chester Jones suddenly appeared in the doorway, fresh from his shower, a towel tied modestly about his waist! They stared at each other, surprised and shocked. At his singular appearance Kate's prepared speech fell to pieces and she stammered out her explanation.

'I was asked to deliver these papers. I understood they were urgent.'

His look of surprise gave way to an amused grin and he combed back his wet hair with his fingers. 'You seem to have caught me unawares ... I thought you were George ... but it seems I made a mistake.'

'So did I,' said Kate drily.

He shrugged a wet, glistening shoulder. 'I'm sorry if my appearance startled you ...' but all attempts to remain serious failed him and he continued to smile.

Kate found his amusement at her embarrassment irksome. 'Don't worry on my account, Mr Jones. I've seen worse.' She thrust the file into his outstretched hand and turned to leave, but despite his size he moved quickly and a muscular arm barred her exit.

'I'm sorry, I didn't intend to be rude.' He looked repentant. 'Would you wait at least until I dress?'

He seemed determined not to let her pass and, unable to move with dignity around his huge frame, Kate allowed herself to be gently led into a large sitting room. He motioned towards a coffee table: 'You'll find some fresh coffee in that pot.'

She sat down on one of two comfortable sofas set before a large open fire. After the orderly sparseness of his office, the warm and welcoming atmosphere of the room was unexpected. Shelves were crowded with books and periodicals. Here and there about the room were individual pieces: a Japanese screen, a marble sculpture from Italy, ivory carvings on a side table. A collection of paintings covered one wall and, to Kate's surprise, a small grand piano sat in front of one of two curved windows. As the recorded strains of a Mozart opera came to a conclusion, she became conscious of the room's incredible quiet, just yards from a main road.

After several moments he reappeared, dressed casually in a brown polo-neck sweater and dark slacks, his feet pushed into soft leather casuals. She watched in silence as he piled logs on to the fire, then turned and spoke.

'Your errand deserves something more than hot coffee.'

He strode towards the sideboard, his long legs moving easily in his own setting, and poured two drinks. As he came forward with their glasses, his eyes slid discreetly over the length of leg Kate was unwittingly showing, seated as she was on a low, deep sofa. He placed her drink before her on the coffee table and keeping his own in his hand, sat in an armchair facing her, his long legs stretched out. She studied her drink, her thoughts refusing to assemble. When she finally looked up and met his gaze there was a glint of amusement in his eyes.

'What are you smiling at?' she asked, colour staining her cheeks.

'Your apparent conviction that I've laced your drink with arsenic.'

Despite herself she laughed goodnaturedly.

'Ah,' he said, 'that's better.' He sipped his drink. 'Do I really appear such a Jekyll and Hyde monster?' His question appeared genuine and, fired by the mixture of the wine and the warm room, her courage grew.

'There are rumours about the office; of frequent absences, strange outbursts behind locked doors. I believe junior buyers have even witnessed the "transition".'

It was his turn now and he threw back his head and laughed out loud.

'And I suppose you and Joanna compare notes over dinner? Here, let me get you some ice.' He picked up her glass and went into the kitchen, continuing their conversation at a distance. 'I couldn't help noticing how much happier Joanna looked the other evening. Your friendship seems to have done her a lot of good.'

'I'm afraid *I* can't take all the credit.'

'No?' There was speculation in his voice, and too late Kate realised he was waiting for her explanation. She made an attempt to speak casually, carefully.

'Simon Forrest was joining us for dinner that evening.'

He frowned as he handed over her drink. 'It didn't take him long to reappear on the scene . . .' He settled himself opposite. 'When things came to a head at Bennett's and Joanna left, he lay low for quite a while. No letter, not even a phone call.'

'Perhaps he was a little wary of the reception he might receive from Big Brother?'

'If he really loved Jo and cared what happened to her that should have made no difference.'

'Maybe they met secretly? Afraid of the fuss you might make.'

He leant forward, resting his elbows on his knees. 'Joanna came pretty close to a nervous breakdown and

I sent her off to relatives in Switzerland for several weeks—months, as it turned out. Any phone call or letter would have had to come through me.' He studied his glass for a moment, lost in thought. 'Forrest was simply looking out for his own skin and at that time he couldn't afford to be seen showing public allegiance to a discredited buyer.'

'Aren't you being a little unjust?' Kate queried.

'His type doesn't deserve justice. He's a man without principles and should be treated as such.'

'That's only your opinion.'

'I wish it were . . . Ask around. Ask anyone who has ever had any dealings with the man . . .'

'Gossip,' Kate said with some contempt. 'You condemn a man on hearsay.'

He shook his head firmly. 'Gossip plays no part in it; the man and his actions speak for themselves.'

'He seems to lead a pretty normal life to my way of thinking.'

'That's another thing; the man's life-style is far in excess of his earnings! Fashion writers simply don't earn that kind of salary.'

'You being in a position to know, of course?' said Kate.

He glanced up quickly, catching her insinuation. 'I take it you mean Erika?'

Kate ran her finger around the edge of her glass. 'Simon's closest rival, wouldn't you say?'

There was quiet irritation in his voice. 'Contrary to what you may have been told, Miss Gibbs has not contributed to the "gossip". As a successful journalist in her own right, she has little or no concern for the likes of Forrest.' He drained his glass with a quick movement. 'Furthermore, she's too much of a professional to dabble in office politics.'

'That's not what I've heard.'

'What you have heard, no doubt, is a highly coloured

version from Joanna, who appears incorrigible in her dislike of Miss Gibbs.'

'Some might describe your own attitude towards Simon Forrest in a similar vein!'

His voice grew louder. 'It's not at all the same thing. Joanna has need of protection, moral as well as financial, whereas I can handle most . . .'

'Women?'

'Situations, was what I was about to say.'

'But you had "women" in mind?'

He gave a sardonic smile. 'If you like . . .'

His arrogant manner both annoyed and disturbed her, but she spoke as coolly as she could manage. 'You don't appear to have had much success with Joanna?'

'Ah, Joanna . . . We appear to have come full circle.' He hesitated. 'I sometimes think that her financial dependence upon me has partly contributed to her problem. She's never really had to stand on her own two feet. Perhaps this legacy will resolve matters, but that won't really amount to much . . .'

'Wouldn't you say her new job was a step in the right direction?'

He shrugged a shoulder. 'You heard her views on that the other evening.'

'How about the flat?'

'I found it and bought the lease. I practically had to push her out of the nest.'

'It seems to have aroused her enthusiasm . . . and hidden talents.'

'I had hoped it would give her a dose of reality.'

'Joanna is a romantic, and maybe reality is just what she doesn't want,' Kate suggested.

He grimaced. 'And as a romantic she's a sitting duck for the likes of Simon Forrest.'

'We can't all be level-headed realists, capable of handling all *situations*.'

'More's the pity. The only reason Joanna and others

can indulge themselves in a whimsical dreamworld is because some level-headed realist provides them with financial security.'

'Perhaps it's not *financial* security she wants . . .'

'What other sort is there?'

'The kind Simon Forrest can probably provide— emotional security.' She ignored his look of contempt. 'Has it ever occurred to you that his feelings might be genuine; that he was thinking in terms of marriage?'

Chester Jones shook his head in mock disbelief.

'But would you be against such a marriage?'

'The matter would simply never arise.'

'And if you were wrong?'

He grunted. 'Now who's the romantic?'

Recognising the warning signs, Kate decided it was time to remove her irritating presence and glanced at her wristwatch. 'It's getting late, I ought to be going.'

He stood up. 'I'll drive you home, of course.'

'There's no need, I'll take a taxi.'

'You've done me a favour this evening, let me do you one. Besides, young ladies do not walk unescorted late at night in this particular corner of London.'

'I'm quite capable of handling any unpleasantness that may arise, Mr Jones.'

'So I recall.'

Kate felt herself redden at this remark and was grateful for the subdued lighting of the foyer.

'If you're sure . . .'

'I'm sure.'

He lifted a shoulder as if it was of no consequence, and as she walked along the corridor and descended the carpeted staircase, he stood leaning against the doorframe, watching her depart.

Pleased at her show of independence, Kate emerged from the warm building into a biting cold wind and immediately regretted her refusal. She had only been walking a few moments when a dark limousine drew into the kerbside, and mindful of Chester's warning Kate stared intently ahead and quickened her pace, her heels brisk on the pavement. She heard the car door open and looked up with a start when she heard her name called. Chester Jones' face was peering out..

'Where did you say you lived?'

His appearance startled her. 'But how . . .?'

He eyed her with amusement. 'Something distantly related to Newton's Law of Gravity; you took the stairs, I took the lift.'

Persuaded more by the harsh elements than by his brusque tone, Kate reluctantly got in, and hardly had she settled back in her seat than the car leapt silently forward.

'Cigarette?'

'No, thank you, I don't smoke.'

He lit himself a cigarette and for a flickering moment the lighter revealed his straight classical nose and determined chin; a strong profile, yet with an air of sensitivity about the high cheekbones and well shaped mouth. A man of contradictions, thought Kate, stealing a glance at the broad shoulders that sat easily in the voluminous leather driving seat.

'Where to?'

Kate directed him towards a leafy avenue off Hampstead Heath. They had ridden in silence, but as the car drew up alongside a row of small neat terrace cottages, Chester stopped the engine and turned towards her, his eyes inscrutable in the darkness.

'How are you liking it with Publicity?' he asked.

'I enjoy working for Christopher . . . very much.'

'That wasn't what I asked.'

'There's a difference?' An edge of defiance crept into her voice. 'For whom I work is as important as the job to be done. Besides, I prefer verbal battles *not* to be part of the office routine. Joanna looks for excitement; I'm content with peaceful co-existence.'

There was a pause, a rather long pause, the steering wheel occupying his attention. 'I'm afraid you caught me on a bad day.'

'My day didn't turn out so well,' she pointed out.

'Molly has been complaining bitterly at your absence, and my part in it.'

'Molly doesn't run the Buying Department.'

He slowly stubbed out his cigarette, not looking at her. 'No, but she has a nasty habit of running me. If you should change your mind, your position is still available. With an increased salary, of course.'

She spoke quietly, coldly. 'Money doesn't resolve every problem, Mr Jones, although some people might believe it to be the panacea for all ills.'

He rubbed his cheek. 'I'm sorry you take it that way. My offer was meant as a compliment.'

'Not all women respond to flattery.'

'Only some, some of the time?'

Something in his tone made her glance sharply in his direction. He reached over and pulled from the glove compartment a glossy trade magazine. Without speaking he drew her attention to the back page and to a small photograph of Simon Forrest with his arm around her shoulders.

'You appear to respond to his particular line of persuasion.'

Feeling her temper rise at what he had read into the photograph and at the implied accusation, Kate threw the magazine aside.

'Men in the fashion trade are either boorishly rude or rudely familiar,' she protested fiercely, 'neither of which I lose very much sleep over.'

'What sort of men do affect your sleep, Miss Whelan?'

Kate blushed at the insinuation contained in the tone of his question, but continued as if he had not spoken.

'You've deliberately misconstrued the picture. We

were at a public reception along with Mr Lloyd and several hundred other invited guests—all perfectly innocent.'

'I can think of many words to describe Forrest, but *innocent* isn't one of them.'

'In that case, what makes you think *I'd* succumb to the likes of Simon Forrest?'

'You're a woman, aren't you?'

She opened the car door and smiled disdainfully over her shoulder. 'I'm surprised you'd even noticed.'

His reply followed her through the open window. 'Nothing much escapes me . . .'

Bristling with anger at the infuriating pomposity of the man, Kate slammed shut the car door and walked towards her house, conscious of his eyes following her. On reaching the porch, she turned and saw the silent car still sitting at the kerb, its silhouetted occupant quietly finishing his cigarette.

CHAPTER SIX

CRICKET headlines had begun to appear smaller and lower down the page, making way for the weightier pronouncements of the football pundits. Holiday snapshots had been developed, sighed over and put away for winter reminiscences. Rested and tanned, most ordinary folk were regretting the inevitable approach of colder weather; for them the month of September signalled the end of summer and all its seasonal pleasures. For retailers, September was the beginning of autumn, the most important season in the fashion calendar, and they welcomed it with barely a backward glance. Three good autumn months and a dismal trading year could end up showing a profit; poor autumn figures and nine months hard work might be of little consequence.

With summer holidays past and paid for, and Christmas still on the distant horizon, a lot of people were walking around with loose change in their pocket and, for the retailer, the task of persuading them to part with this surplus was twofold; to create a consumer need for warm and expensive winter outfits and then to secure customer allegiance at the beginning of the season. Getting customers to spend was the easy part; getting them into the store—to leave warm beds, warm offices, be jostled and crushed on public transport and *then* into the store, and making it all appear worthwhile—was the responsibility and headache of the Publicity Department. Arrangements were made for Kate to launch her fashion promotion at the beginning of September at Bennett's influential West End store and thereafter the provincial branches.

Persuasive literature a week beforehand and a small

free sherry on the day had filled up every chair by six o'clock, and with lots of backstage grins and encouragement Kate took her place at the centre of the platform and began her commentary. Several rehearsals and close attention to detail ensured a smooth performance, and hearing the murmur of excitement as each new outfit made its appearance, Kate felt a wave of relief after all the hard work, as well as pleasure at the enthusiastic response from the audience.

After several weeks of touring with her fashion troupe her supply of throat pastilles had substantially diminished and she was pleased to return to the peaceful turbulence of her own office. A message to call Tom Preston lay on her desk.

'Kate, we've organised a party for Molly tomorrow evening. Eight o'clock at Parsons. Can you make it?'

'What's the occasion?' she asked.

'It's her silver anniversary. She's been with Bennett's twenty-five years.'

'Twenty-five years!' echoed Kate.

'So we can't be all bad, right?'

'Maybe . . . but I'll let you know for sure when I collect *my* silver dish,' laughed Kate.

'Can you make it?' asked Tom. 'I'm trying to organise the drinks.'

'I'm having to visit Brighton tomorrow with Christopher, but we should be back in good time.'

'I'll be seeing you, then. Let Chris know the times . . .'

He rang off before she had a chance to mention Chester Jones. Kate had not seen him since that strange encounter at his flat; several weeks of travel, hers provincial, his of a more exotic nature, had kept them both moving in opposite directions, but she supposed he would be attending the party. She toyed with the idea of feigning sickness, but for Molly's sake she decided otherwise. There were certain to be lots of people there and she could easily avoid coming face to face with him—after all, there was anonymity as well as safety in numbers.

'I suppose you've heard all the fuss,' said Molly with mock resignation, as she shared a crowded lift with Kate later that evening.

'Twenty-five years with the same company *is* something of a track record,' observed Kate.

'But hardly an occasion to cause the champagne to flow,' Molly grimaced. 'It's bound to put Geoffrey off if he gets to hear of it.' Geoffrey was Molly's latest beau.

'Would you like us to pick you up tomorrow?' asked Kate. 'Christopher has promised me a lift.'

'Please. Tom's threatened me with star billing and I'm going to be in need of strong moral support. You know what he's like! With other people it's the drink that goes to their head, with Tom it's the occasion.' The evening was grey and damp and Molly hailed a passing taxi. 'Can I give you a lift somewhere?'

Kate shook her head. 'No, thanks, I've a theatre date.' She waved goodbye. 'Don't forget to have your hair done, the trade press are bound to be there.'

Molly gave a groan. 'Oh, the public shame of twenty-five years!' As the taxi began to move off she wound down her window. 'Couldn't you give my excuses?'

Kate grinned. 'We'll collect you at seven-thirty sharp.'

At twenty-five minutes past eight Christopher deposited Kate and Molly outside Parsons' dilapidated entrance. Kate had long suspected that the club's slight air of decadence was deliberately maintained by the management in order to discourage passing trade, and so retain exclusivity for those people in the fashion business who regularly gathered there to talk shop. Their needs were simple and, given a place and opportunity to exchange gossip and headaches with like-minded men and women, they made no aesthetic demands on their club premises. Surroundings were inconsequential compared to the two thoughts uppermost in their mind and on their lips—'How's business?' and 'Who's doing it?'

'Not bad timing, all things considered,' said Christopher as he helped them out of the car.

'I just didn't feel right in that blue outfit,' Molly sighed.

He grinned. 'Nor the grey or the beige?'

She tapped him playfully on his shoulder. 'It's the likes of me that keep the likes of you in business, young man!'

Christopher smiled goodnaturedly and offered an arm. 'I suppose Kate would call it market research.'

He led the way through a dark side passage and up a narrow flight of stairs to the room traditionally reserved for such occasions. As they entered heads turned in their direction and a beaming Tom Preston held his arms wide in welcome. 'At last! We've been waiting to start the celebrations.' He motioned over a waiter. 'Champagne for starters okay?' He took three of the proffered glasses from the waiter and handed them over.

Drink and smoke circulated about the warm room and the chatter of people intent on enjoying themselves filled the air.

'The world and its wife appears to have turned up,' commented Christopher, arching his back to let a couple pass.

'Plus the usual freeloaders.' Tom motioned his head in no particular direction. 'They can smell a free drink bars away!'

After the cold wet evening, the room, always a trifle gloomy during the day, had an unexpectedly cosy appearance: pink wall lights, dusty relics of a more elegant decade, had a kindly effect on the faded furnishings and fittings that showed their age in the harsher light of day. The less young and the not so pretty felt younger and prettier in the soft lights, and Kate, for neither of those reasons, also felt pleased with the shadows. Two long tables overflowed with glasses and bottles in the centre of the room, while a smaller side table offered a limited selection of cheese and ham sandwiches. Obviously, Tom's dutiful preoccupation with the former had left him little time for the latter, thought Kate with some amusement.

As later arrivals noisily demanded Tom's presence and attention, Molly turned to her companions. 'I think I ought to circulate. Would you excuse me?' As she spoke a distinguished-looking gentleman detached himself from a group and came forward to embrace her.

'Darling, you look ravishing! Why has it been so long?'

Smiling and offering apologies, Molly moved away.

Left alone with Christopher, Kate sipped her drink and glanced around the room. She was on good terms with a lot of the people there, but just then she felt the need of Christopher's reassuring presence, and besides, his friendly and attentive manner made him pleasant company as well as giving her morale a boost. She had taken special care over her appearance that evening; her hair was smooth and shining, her skin glowed and her red knitted dress, though deceptively simple, was superbly cut to show every curve, and had drawn forth a whistle of appreciation from Christopher.

When Christopher left to park his car, several young men turned to include her in their sphere of conversation, and soon Kate was enjoying their noisy good humour and the inevitable 'shop' gossip. The pithy conclusion of one particular story brought forth a lot of laughter, and it was then she became aware of a figure on the edge of her vision. Turning her head towards a nearby group, she caught the intense stare of Chester Jones and for several moments he held her gaze until a question claimed her attention.

Feeling uncomfortable at having been an object of appraisal, Kate excused herself and moved down the room away from his line of vision. She wondered vaguely about the girl he had been talking to; the lights had been too low to catch more than the barest detail of her face. As she made her way through the laughter and smoke, she caught sight of Molly talking happily away to an attentive listener; in the distance Ken Baldwin, Bennett's window dresser supremo, appeared to be the cause of much amusement, while elsewhere one of Tom's lengthy stories held a captive audience. Suddenly Kate felt an inexplicable urge to get away, away from all that jollity and she edged towards large windows that led to a small balcony.

A fresh breeze lifted her hair as she leant her elbows on the crumbling stone parapet and surveyed the narrow street below; the rain earlier in the evening had stopped and the pavements glistened in the dark. A dismal street that thronged with fashion buyers and cloth merchants throughout the day, but was now deserted save for a few hurrying figures intent on their destination. Dustbins and boxes overflowed with lengths of discarded fabric; unsold stock that no manufacturer could afford to accumulate in an area where square footage was at a premium, and which would eventually serve as warm bedding for the derelicts who loitered each night among the debris. A sad reflection on the glossy world portrayed by the elegant windows one block away, thought Kate sadly as she gave a little shiver.

'I get the impression you don't much care for these occasions?'

At the sudden intrusion upon her thoughts her heart jumped and she turned to face Chester Jones. He stood in the doorway, silhouetted against the light in the room.

'Whatever makes you think that?' She spoke calmly, although her pulses were racing.

He took his time lighting a cigarette. 'Your necklace.'

'My necklace?' Kate frowned and her fingers felt for the slender gold chain she always wore about her neck.

He flicked shut his lighter. 'Some people quell their anxiety with drink, others clutch at something familiar.'

Quietly amazed at how close he had come to a home truth, she said nothing, then a slight smile lifted the corners of her mouth. 'So much better than smoking, wouldn't you say?'

In the half light she fancied his eyes returned her smile. 'Healthier . . .' She leant back against the balcony. 'You're right, of course. Large gatherings of people intent on enjoying themselves have always made me nervous.'

'I also appear to make you nervous,' he commented.

'You?' She attempted a laugh. 'Whatever makes you . . .' Quickly she pulled her hand away from the gold chain, wondering how many times in the past her personal mannerism had betrayed her. 'I see I shall have to wear high-necked sweaters in future!'

She felt her cheeks burn as he stood looking at her for some time, without speaking, then he said: 'Have you given any thought to my offer?'

'Was I meant to?'

'Do you always treat offers of promotion in such a cavalier manner?'

'Only since I was *demoted* in a cavalier manner . . . You might say I haven't fully recovered from the shock.'

'Or your vanity hasn't,' he suggested.

'Possibly . . .'

'You must know that your talents are wasted in Publicity,' he told her.

'Is that what Publicity thinks?'

'It's what I think. As head of the buying department, naturally my first concern is to establish a strong buying team, and you're a good buyer.'

'And Publicity. Isn't that important?'

'Important, yes, but not *that* important. The right merchandise will always sell, eventually. No amount of ballyhoo will sell the mistakes.'

'What about all those graduate trainees waiting in the wings?' asked Kate.

'Mere paper qualifications. You can't *teach* style.'

She frowned, recalling their first meeting. 'You seem to have changed your mind about me since our first meeting.'

'I've seen your success in Publicity, seen that Publicity's gain has been my loss.'

'Then why transfer me if the job I like doing, I'm doing well?'

'Because as a buyer you'd be worth a whole lot more.'

'Thank you for being so blunt,' she said coldly.

He spoke in a quiet voice. 'I understood you didn't go in for flattery.'

'There are ways and ways of telling a girl she's needed, or should I take your honesty as a compliment?'

'Take it how you will. It's the truth.' His eyes narrowed as he drew deeply on his cigarettes. 'No doubt there are plenty of boy-friends to supply you with the social niceties . . .'

She refused to satisfy his curiosity, and in the ensuing silence a voice called: 'There you are, darling!' and a strikingly handsome girl with an abundance of auburn hair stepped forward. Laying a hand with long polished nails on his arm, she threw Kate a brief hostile glance that took in every detail of her appearance. 'We're all waiting for the presentation.'

'Erika, have you met Kate Whelan? She works for Publicity, but I've just been trying to persuade her to return to the Buying Department . . .'

Erika Gibbs cut across his explanation with more than a hint of impatience.

'Chester, it really is rude of us to keep Molly waiting.'

'Molly's waited twenty-five years, I don't suppose she'll mind a few minutes more.' He smiled at Kate apologetically. 'Would you excuse me?'

Motioning to the auburn temptress to precede him through the narrow doorway, he turned back for a moment, his smile lingering. 'I'd like to have your decision as soon as possible.'

To Kate's surprise Chester Jones turned out to be an accomplished speaker. Laughter filled the room at his droll asides, and Kate could not help but be impressed at the ease with which he handled himself and the occasion. After Molly's tearful acceptance of his public appreciation and a beautiful silver tea service, Kate looked at her wristwatch and wondered if she might decently leave. Weeks with the travelling circus had left her sorely in need of an early night, and cigarette smoke was beginning to sting her eyes. She felt a tap on her shoulder and turned to face Molly.

'What were you and Chester so busily discussing out there?' the other woman asked.

Kate told her of Chester Jones' offer.

'What will you do?' asked Molly.

'I don't know,' Kate replied honestly. 'Playing musical chairs wouldn't exactly enhance my professional reputation.'

'Aren't you ever so slightly tempted by the salary increase?'

'Of course I am, but it's not that simple. I do owe some allegiance to Christopher. He did me the good turn, remember.'

'As it's turned out, he did himself a good turn,' Molly pointed out. 'You've done wonders in Publicity—woken them all up!'

'There is such a thing as professional loyalty,' Kate reminded her.

'Sentiment has no place in business; men know that from the cradle, women always have to learn it—usually the hard way.'

'I suspect if our positions were reversed you'd think exactly like me.'

Molly shrugged. 'Maybe, but then I've always steered well clear of any emotional entanglement in business.'

'Emotional entanglement?' Kate looked at her with surprise. 'I don't see where emotions come into it—unless you include Chester Jones' temper!'

'There was quite an emotional hornets' nest stirred up this evening.' Kate looked blankly at Molly. 'Erika almost blew her top when she discovered that you and Chester were deep in conversation outside . . . I wouldn't have missed it for the world.'

Kate stared at Molly as if she was suffering from a temporary case of mental derangement. 'But it was all perfectly innocent! I told you, we were talking business. It was only a matter of minutes.'

'You and I know that, but Erika thought otherwise,' smiled Molly knowingly. 'Given a beautiful girl and a moonlit balcony, not many men would choose to discuss business . . . You can imagine the conclusion Erika came to.'

Kate threw up her hands in mock horror. 'Heaven help me if anyone else came to a similar one! His cussedness I can just about handle. His friendship I need like a hole in the head.'

'From where I stood, I'd say Erika thought precisely the same.'

'A woman as beautiful as Erika Gibbs has no need to worry about competition.'

Molly gave a dismissive wave of her hand. 'Just a lot of window dressing. If you ask me, Chester . . .' She started to say something further, then hesitated when she saw the subject of their discussion approaching. His mouth was set in a hard line and when he spoke his voice was brusque.

'Could I have a word with you, Molly?'

Appearing not to notice Kate's presence, he piloted Molly away and towards a corner of the room.

Somewhat bemused by the evening's turn of events, Kate decided to look for Christopher. Dear sensible Christopher with two size tens firmly planted on the ground floor; nothing mysterious or untoward in his behaviour. All around her drink had begun to take its inevitable toll; conversation was no longer lighthearted, voices had become loud and boorish, confidences indiscriminate. As Kate looked anxiously about the room for Christopher, her eyes were drawn in Chester Jones' direction. He had his back to her, but Molly's expression left Kate in no doubt that a lighthearted tête-à-tête was precisely what they were not having either.

Christopher's lean appearance broke her reverie. 'Do you want a lift home? I've an early start tomorrow and some reports to catch up on beforehand ...' She nodded, relieved at the opportunity to get away. 'See you outside in ten minutes. I have to collect the car.'

As he walked away Molly appeared at her elbow and drew her to one side. 'Chester's in a terrible rage. Apparently Simon and Joanna are engaged. Erika broke the glad tidings to him this evening, bless her—she's friendly with a secretary in Simon's office.'

Kate pursed her lips. 'Hardly the time and place for such a revelation. No wonder he looked angry!'

'More shocked than angry,' Molly corrected.

'You're right—compared to the storm I first encountered he appeared almost becalmed.'

'Chester's like a time bomb. The moment to worry is when you can't hear the ticking.' There was fleeting speculation in Molly's eyes. 'Did *you* know of their plans?'

'Joanna did speak of an engagement,' Kate admitted,

'but I thought it more wishful thinking. She didn't even have a ring, and having heard Simon's views on the state of matrimony I was sceptical of it ever taking place.'

Molly grimaced. 'Unfortunately Chester thinks you were part of the dastardly scheme.'

Kate stared at Molly in amazement. 'What an interpretation to put upon my friendship with Joanna!'

'He says you put up quite a spirited defence on Forrest's behalf the other evening.'

'That's hardly surprising. Anything that man opposes I'd automatically defend to the death.'

'He believes they asked you to promote their cause with him.'

'A devil's advocate?' asked Kate.

'Something like that.'

'I should be grateful he hasn't accused me of witchcraft, eye of newt and tail of toad in his drink,' said Kate angrily.

'Darling, don't get carried away,' said Molly in a conciliatory tone, 'you know toads don't have tails . . . By the way, what did he mean by "the other evening"?'

Kate waved a hand. 'It was all a terrible mistake. I had to deliver some urgent papers to an address, offices I thought, only it turned out to be Chester Jones' flat.'

'Well, he thinks it was all contrived. That you had dinner with Joanna and Simon and arranged to drop by accidentally.'

'The man's a fool! How dare he presume . . .'

Molly put her hand on Kate's arm in a pacifying gesture. 'I'm on your side, remember? Save your defence for the prosecution. I just thought I'd let you know what you're up against. After a good night's sleep he'll probably think otherwise.'

As Molly resumed her social duties, Kate collected her coat and made her way towards the entrance to wait for Christopher. The slight breeze had become a biting wind and she pulled her collar up round her ears.

Outwardly calm, she burnt with an intense anger; anger at her own lack of foresight at ever having become embroiled in Joanna's tempestuous relationships in the first place. As she stood in the shadows she heard footsteps descending the wooden stairs and hurrying along the unlit corridor. Deep in his thoughts and staring straight ahead, she saw Chester Jones before he saw her, and as he drew alongside she spoke, not really knowing what to say.

'Molly told me . . .'

Suddenly made aware of her presence, he didn't give her a chance to finish. 'What the hell do you think you're playing at, Miss Whelan?'

'I don't know what you mean?'

'Molly told *you*. Weren't you in a position to tell *me*?'

'It wasn't like that . . .' She floundered. How could she explain away the apparent deceit?

'You were with Joanna the other evening. Did she or did she not tell you of her engagement plans?' he asked, his face grim.

'Well, yes, but I thought . . .'

'You should have left the thinking to me, Miss Whelan. I might have dissuaded her.'

'But it wasn't like that. She didn't even have a ring . . . and besides, I gave my word not to say anything. Would you expect me to betray that trust?'

His voice was strained and furious. 'You betrayed mine without much soul-searching.'

'Yours?'

A muscle twitched in his jaw. 'As I'm your employer don't you owe me some loyalty?'

She flung him a look of pure hate. 'You may have bought my time, but not me!' she snapped.

'I wouldn't be so certain of that, young lady.'

During their heated exchange a slim figure had quietly approached and stood listening, and as Chester Jones turned on his heel and strode away Erika Gibbs gave

Kate a thin smile of veiled satisfaction before she
followed in his footsteps. Several minutes later the
engine of a dark limousine roared to life and drove off.

Once home, Kate slipped off the red dress she had worn
and lay down on the bed. In the darkness a sense of
heavy weariness crept over her as she stared unseeingly
at the shadows that patterned the bedroom ceiling. She
lay there for a long time without moving, thinking over
the evening's events. After a while she fumbled around
with an outstretched hand and switched on her bedside
light. The tear-stained face that peered back at her in
her dressing table mirror was bare of the make-up she
had applied earlier that evening, and she thought of the
sophisticated Erika; eyelashes and lipstick still in place
at the end of the evening. Her own flushed cheeks were
smooth and clear, and freckles trickled across her small
nose; a childlike face that sat ingenuously upon a
woman's full-bloom body. Kate wrinkled her nose at
her full breast above a tiny waist as she thought of
Erika's sylphlike proportions. 'Damn Simon Forrest,'
she said aloud. 'Damn and blast him!'

CHAPTER SEVEN

DESPITE the inevitable delay at Heathrow and now the taxi's bumpy suspension, Kate smiled happily out of the window, pleased to be back in Paris so soon. It was still early morning, but as they drove through the narrow winding streets to their hotel, the emerging workaday world of Parisian life had an atmosphere and charm all of its own. Everything seemed so much better than she had remembered; familiarity might have dulled her senses, but not her excitement.

The night after her heated exchange with Chester Jones she had fallen asleep consumed with hatred of the man and all he stood for, but morning had dawned with cold reality and her anger gave way to a more positive approach. Not for a second time would she jeopardise her position at work; to lose one job over Joanna might be considered a little foolhardy, to lose two would be thoroughly unprofessional. She determined to put the whole affair out of her mind and concentrate her energies on the work in hand.

Before long she was up to her elbows in plans and promotions, thriving on the bustle and urgency that invariably attended all publicity campaigns. Suitably impressed by her subsequent results and talent for presenting a 'story', Christopher called her into his office late one afternoon, pleased to be the bearer of good news. 'I thought you'd like to know that arrangements have been made for you to attend the Pret-à-Porter collections in Paris,' he told her.

At the mention of France, Kate frowned. 'I thought only buyers saw the collections?'

'Usually, but we've plans for a new French department and Chester thinks it important that someone from Publicity goes along to pick up a few promotional ideas . . . I'd go myself, but he wants me to attend an opening in Bristol on his behalf.'

'He thinks *someone* from Publicity should go?' Kate pursed her lips. 'I feel sure he wouldn't want that someone to be me.'

Christopher shrugged. 'He specifically asked for you. Said you've an eye for style and mood.'

Surprise, then anxiety registered on Kate's face. 'That's not what he said the other day.'

'Don't be petulant. It's not everyone who's personally recommended by the boss. You should be flattered.'

In future, Kate thought to herself, life would be simpler if she resisted all temptation to try and understand the perverse workings of Chester Jones' mind.

Twice yearly, an air of barely controlled excitement hung about the buying offices as preparations were made to converge on Paris for the ready-to-wear exhibition. Noisy enthusiasm from the younger travellers; mouthings of boredom from the more jaded buyers, but once the form-filling and packing were completed, the early morning touch down at de Gaulle airport never failed to put everyone in high spirits. Hotel bookings had been handled by Chester Jones' personal secretary and consequently the accommodation was a distinct improvement on Kate's previous visit. Their taxi drew up outside a tall elegant building in the Rue du Faubourg-St Honoré. 'This is more like it!' whispered Molly, as a commissionaire discreetly materialised and bowed them in through the glass doors.

They presented themselves to a slightly harassed receptionist who consulted her book, smiled and handed them their keys. In spite of the early hour small groups of men and women stood about the reception area talking, and as Kate and Molly moved towards the lift a young man broke away from one of the groups and came towards them, both hands extended. 'Molly! It's good to see you again,' he smiled, his accent complementing his Gallic features.

Alain Boivin was not tall, dark and handsome, but he was tall and he was most attractive. Molly introduced Kate and they shook hands, and when he smiled she saw that his eyes were very blue and looked with approval on the fair young Englishwoman. Monsieur Boivin was employed by Bennett's to be their eyes and ears in Paris. Each month typed reports bearing his signature would land on every buyer's desk, summarising the current trends and promotions in France. During their visits to France he would introduce manufacturers and wholesalers who might be of interest to English buyers and should business entail, it was his job to interpret the small print on French contracts and, in general, save the London office a lot of headaches.

'I was hoping you'd join me for breakfast.'

Molly glanced at her watch and frowned. 'I'd like to, but I'd also like to make an early start.'

'There's a lot we have to discuss beforehand. Why not over coffee?'

'Let's compromise and have coffee in our suite. The rest of the buyers should be along soon and it will save you having to see each of us in turn.'

He shrugged his shoulders and smiled. 'I should not mind if they were all as beautiful as yourself and Mademoiselle Whelan.'

A large ornate suite overlooking a quiet courtyard had been reserved for Molly's party. There were a number of small bedrooms leading off from the spacious sitting room that was filled with the usual selection of polished hotel furniture as well as several comfortable sofas.

With something akin to shock, Kate had learned from Molly on the flight over that Chester Jones was travelling direct to Paris from Munich and was to share their suite of rooms. Apparently this was usual procedure on overseas trips to Paris, when at this time of the year demand for single rooms far outstripped the supply and, as Molly wryly pointed out, communication was so much easier if everybody was within shouting distance, 'Particularly if the boss can't speak a word of the language!'

With reluctance Kate acknowledged the practical advantages of such an arrangement, understood even, but understanding didn't help. Chester Jones sleeping across the way! She felt her cheeks flush at the image that conjured up and hoped Molly hadn't noticed. Molly had.

'Don't worry. He usually only stays for one night . . .'

As soon as the rest of the buyers had arrived and the usual grumbles about French taxis disposed of, Alain ordered coffee and croissants from room service and adopted a more businesslike tone. Aware that time was at a premium and that everybody present was anxious to breathe real Parisian exhaust fumes, he spoke briefly and to the point.

He suggested they gave their first day over to the Exhibition. 'It's increased in size since your last visit and takes a lot of time to cover all the floors thoroughly.' He handed out to each buyer a map and a typed list of names. 'These are new companies established since your last visit. I've underlined those I think deserve a second look. My secretary has also drawn up a list of the more interesting boutiques around the city and marked them on the map.'

After dealing with several requests for directions from the newer buyers, he gave a general outline of the itinerary he had planned for the remainder of their trip, and by the time the waiter had appeared with a tray of fresh hot coffee, the meeting had been concluded and the attractive Frenchman was preparing to leave. 'If you have any problems my telephone number is at the foot of the list, and tomorrow I shall be entirely at your disposal.' He turned to go, then changed his mind. 'I almost forgot. Mr Jones has asked me to join you all for dinner this evening . . .' Murmurs of approval met the news and he smiled to the room in general and then to Kate in particular. 'I, too, look forward to that pleasure.'

The combination of blue eyes and French charm might well compensate her having to spend her first evening in Paris with her tyrannical employer, reflected Kate.

Despite a dull start, the day had turned out crisp and sunny and an air of anticipation hung about the long queue outside the Porte de Versailles. Buyers waiting expectantly, their tickets clasped in their hands. In the past some might have quietly expressed doubts, others spoken aloud, of the declining influence of Paris fashion, but when summoned few could resist. In a world that regularly reverberated to the sound of fashion houses crumbling to the ground, for the sake of a day's head-line, the press continued to seek out and publicly applaud the extravagant and spectacular. Against that same background of economic gloom and plunging trade figures, buyers searched for commercial sense; the winning equation of style and colour that would gua-rantee them increased sales and a job for the next six months.

The queue moved steadily through the main entrance and before long Kate and Molly had passed through the ticket barrier and into the main hall. There, the whole spectrum of fashion lay before them like some grand theatrical production with a cast of thousands; rack upon rack of beautiful clothes, decorative models moving to music and lights, slim-hipped salesmen glibly extolling the virtues of their wares, each with a plot to unfold and an audience to listen, salesmen talking en-thusiastically, buyers smiling politely, one step forward, two steps back. It was early days and everyone was overflowing with high spirits. It was a mood hard to resist.

Molly and Kate had decided beforehand to go their separate ways once inside the hall and to meet up later at an arranged time to compare notes. Faced with an inexhaustible range of merchandise, Kate lost no time in working methodically through the rails of garments, noting the recurring shapes and colours; styles ranged from the provincially dull to the startlingly original. As she sat watching a display of knitted separates in bright zingy colours her attention was drawn to a tall slim girl strolling languidly towards the platform; her slight air of disdain out of place with the bustle and excitement of her surroundings.

At first Kate did not recognise Erika Gibbs, whose abundant red hair had disappeared into a small knot on the top of her head. She hoped that the fashion journalist might not have seen her, but with a thin smile of recognition Erika pushed her way through the crowds and slipped into the empty seat next to Kate. Beautifully groomed, her make-up immaculate, she appeared the epitome of a successful career woman, and although the upswept hairstyle was a little too severe for her angular face, it drew attention to her attractive green eyes. At one time Kate had supposed Erika Gibbs to be about her own age, but now, under the harsh strip lighting, she realised she had been mistaken.

'Isn't this heat dreadful?' said Erika, with an air of long-suffering patience. She passed the back of her hand across her forehead. 'Each year it's the same. You'd think they'd do something about it.'

'Why don't you leave your coat in the cloakroom?'

Erika raised her eyebrows. 'You're suggesting I leave *this* in a cloakroom?' A well manicured hand stroked a grey fox fur thrown casually about her shoulders.

'Perhaps not,' conceded Kate with a smile, and

wondered why, if it was 'always the same', Erika came dressed for a snowstorm.

'Don't you find it such a bore trying to do business in these crowds?' continued Erika. 'Everyone jostling for space.'

'I'm simply an observer on this trip, trying to piece together a few commercial stories.'

'My job precisely, only *I* regard that as hard work and I'll be glad when it's all over for another six months.'

'Oh, I don't know . . . I'm quite enjoying myself, crowds and all. It adds to the excitement.'

'Excitement? When you've been as often as I have the element of excitement becomes more and more elusive. For the umpteenth time Paris is either dropping the hemline or revising the mini, while back home a hysterical editor is screaming at you to meet impossible deadlines.'

'You sound very cynical,' commented Kate.

Erika bent down to inspect her boots. 'Possibly because my feet are killing me in these new shoes.' As she smiled she showed small neat teeth that protruded slightly and gave her an attractive pout.

When the display had finished, Erika waited beside the platform while Kate exchanged a few words with one of the salesmen. She was smaller than Kate, but her upswept hairstyle and boyishly slim figure made her appear taller. Beneath her fur coat she wore the type of outfit usually featured on the pages of glossy magazines and in the rarefied atmosphere of Bond Street boutiques, but never really taken seriously elsewhere because of its price and exclusivity. Erika Gibbs was a woman with expensive tastes . . .

'You must excuse me, Erika,' she said, 'but I have to cover a few miles of rails this morning.'

'Oh, don't mind me. I'll just stroll alongside. It helps to see it all through fresh eyes and I did promise Chester to work more closely with his Publicity Department . . .'

Kate felt herself in a Catch 22 situation; either she bore with Erika's company for the rest of the morning or she politely objected and Chester would be told of his 'unco-operative employee'. Her Paris trip was turning out less pleasurable than she had hoped; Big Brother in the evening, his paramour this morning. She could tell it was going to be one of those days . . .

'I understand your boss has given Paris a miss this year,' said Erika.

'Christopher? Yes, he had to attend a branch opening.'

'I was meaning Chester.'

'Chester Jones?' Kate looked puzzled. 'I understood he was flying direct from Munich. He made arrangements to meet Molly here . . . today . . .'

The look that crossed Erika's face was fleeting, but it was one Kate had seen before; that evening on the balcony when Erika had interrupted her conversation with Chester Jones.

'Chester rang when I was out and left a message . . . my secretary must have misheard. You know what these temps are.' She smiled, her composure and reputation once more intact. 'How do you like working for Chester?'

Aware that anything incriminating would be passed on, Kate was noncommittal. 'I don't have any dealings with him now. Christopher is my immediate superior.'

'Poor old Christopher. Not exactly a ball of fire, is he?'

Annoyed as she was at having to bear with the girl's company, this spiteful remark only served to increase Kate's anger. 'He's not on a permanent ego trip, if that's what you mean.'

'Oh, don't get me wrong, personally I think Christopher's a pet, but as Publicity Manager he should be more of a trailblazer.'

'As Publicity Manager he does his job efficiently and well. He's also very considerate towards his staff.'

Erika pulled a face. 'Sounds very dull.'

'You think so? For me it makes a pleasant change.'

'From Chester, you mean?' Kate shrugged, but said nothing, uncertain of how much Erika knew. 'You and he don't appear to get along very well?'

'I find his guerilla tactics in the office not only time-consuming, but thoroughly infantile.'

'But never dull?'

'I'm certain Attila the Hun's wife never complained about the monotony of *her* life, but that's no re-commendation. Although I suppose there are some women who might get a thrill out of such childish behaviour . . .'

Erika threw Kate a sharp, sideways glance, but the latter was past caring where her verbal darts were land-ing, wishing only to be rid of her irritating companion, but Erika Gibbs, ex-sleuth reporter, was not so easily dismissed.

'Chester's not nearly as grim as he'd have you believe. A little sugar and he soon comes to heel.'

Cringing at this piece of feminine folklore, Kate peered hopelessly about for Molly, regretting their decision to work alone.

'Have you heard from Joanna lately?' Erika went on. 'I daren't raise the subject with Chester . . .'

Why not use a little sugar? thought Kate irritably. For a successful businessman Chester Jones appeared to surround himself with remarkably foolish women. If he *were* unwilling to discuss the matter of his sister with Erika, how much less would he want her discussing it with Kate, or was this show of stupidity simply a ploy of Erika's to catch her unaware? Kate decided to tread very carefully. 'I will never understand what it is she sees in Simon Forrest . . . where the attraction lies.'

'Oh, I don't know. Simon gives the impression of

being a man of the world, and men of the world, as a type, have always held a fascination for young girls.'

'Impression is right, the shadow rather than the substance . . . and Joanna is still very young. He's a friend of yours, isn't he?'

'Not a friend exactly, more of a business acquaintance.'

'A smooth operator, don't you think?'

Kate did think so, but had no intention of appearing to side with Erika on this particular issue. 'I suppose it goes with the job. After all, he does work for a very influential newspaper.'

'Influential? With whom? The gilt-edged minority. I'm afraid that in the rag trade it's quantity that counts, not quality.'

Kate was surprised at the girl's supercilious attitude, but then Erika would not suspect her of knowing about her bid for Simon's job. Much to Kate's relief Molly's anxious face suddenly appeared between a rail of dresses. 'I'm trying to lose a boring Dutch manufacturer who wants me to have lunch with him. Any sign of a redheaded leprechaun with horn-rimmed glasses?'

Kate looked about her and gave the all clear. 'You have a habit of collecting strange gentlemen,' she remarked.

'Strange is the word,' said Molly, stepping through the dresses, 'and time's too precious on these trips.' She gave a knowing smile. 'Now if he were of the French vintage . . .' She shrugged her shoulders. 'Kate appears to have more success in that field.' Erika raised a quizzical eyebrow. 'Alain Boivin, our French agent, has taken a tumble for her.

Kate groaned goodnaturedly and changed the subject, and as the three exchanged trivialities her attention was drawn towards a group of people deep in conversation. Even as she looked a tall familiar figure turned suddenly and caught sight of her over his companion's shoulder.

Excusing himself, Chester Jones walked over to meet them.

Kate felt suddenly apprehensive as she recalled their last meeting, but he appeared to be in good spirits.

'Molly—Miss Whelan.' He greeted them with a smile of recognition, but as Erika turned to face him a frown flitted across his face. 'Erika! I thought most of the press came yesterday?'

Surprise lingered on his face and a faint flush appeared on hers. 'My editor wanted to know what the buyers were putting their money on. Besides,' she added almost defensively, 'you're always telling me to work more closely with the retail element.'

He gave her a sharp, wordless glance, then turned his attention to Molly. 'What do you think of the merchandise so far, Molly?'

As Molly spoke he listened with head bowed, hands thrust in the pockets of his jacket. With good reason Kate had learned to mistrust this languid exterior he assumed; he was a man who missed nothing and questioned everything, a hard-headed man of business who thrived on bustle and fast decisions and for the first time, she noticed the flecks of silver around his temples and small lines at the corner of his eyes. He looked up unexpectedly and caught her glance; there was the hint of a smile in his eyes and she smiled back, relieved that the crisis was over. He looked at his wristwatch. 'I'm famished. Are you ready for something to eat?'

Molly smiled apologetically. 'I'm afraid I shall have to skip lunch if I'm to cover the whole exhibition . . .'

'Miss Whelan?'

'Molly's right. There's still a fair amount to see.'

Erika smiled provocatively and settled the fur coat about her shoulders. 'That leaves me, and I'm starving!'

CHAPTER EIGHT

It was late afternoon when they returned to their hotel room and Kate sank thankfully into one of the easy chairs, pleasantly exhausted. She smiled her appreciation as Molly picked up the phone and ordered fresh coffee from room service.

'How I wish I spoke French as well as you,' said Kate enviously.

Molly waved a dismissive hand. 'In any language you need know only two words, *coffee* and *ladies*, the rest is downhill.' She reached into her handbag and took out a cigarette and lighter. 'Of course, a little local male colour helps ... that goes without saying.'

'Mm,' said Kate, not entirely convinced.

'I can't tempt you?' Molly waved the unlit cigarette. 'Or is there someone back home?'

'Nobody serious ... at least, not as far as I'm concerned.'

'Sounds interesting?'

'Not very ... a childhood sweetheart. Philip and I grew up together—went to the same grammar school, and everyone had always assumed that we'd marry. He was doing well as a trainee accountant and the way things were going, we might have married almost because it was expected of us.'

'That would have been tragic,' commented Molly.

'But then I upped and came to London—since when I've had time for dates and fun, but no serious involvements.'

'Take my advice,' said Molly, suddenly serious, 'make time! Look at our male colleagues. Most of them found time to marry.'

'And divorce!'

'You're much too young to be so cynical.'

'Simply observant,' said Kate, leaning back against the cushions and shutting her eyes.

Just then the waiter arrived with a tray of steaming brown coffee and, motioning Kate to remain seated, Molly attended first to the former with a smile and a tip and then to the coffee. Not for the first time, Kate could not help but admire the older woman's reserves of energy. 'All a matter of correct breathing and posture,' was Molly's standard reply to any such observation.

'Chester didn't appear too happy to see Erika?' queried Molly, handing Kate her cup of coffee.

'No,' said Kate vaguely.

Molly shook her head. 'He's a stickler for keeping business and pleasure separate.'

'Erika's his pleasure?'

'So she would have us believe.'

'You think the feeling's not mutual?'

'Let's just say it wouldn't be the first time a woman's done all the running,' Molly smiled. 'I've done it myself once or twice in the past ... if the man was worth catching.'

'It doesn't seem to bother him,' commented Kate.

'Having ladies in frantic pursuit? I can't imagine that bothering any man. I suppose it boosts their ego.'

'Well, I think it reveals a sense of inadequacy,' said Kate scornfully. 'A man in his position should know better.'

Molly laughed out loud. 'My dear Kate, one of life's tragedies is that they never do ... And after all, he can't help looking that good. It's not his fault.'

'It is his fault that he behaves so callously.'

'Callously? Aren't you being a little harsh? It doesn't worry him and it doesn't appear to worry them ... so where's the harm? I've worked with Chester for ten long years and in that time you get to know a lot about a person. I know that when the right one comes along, Erika and the rest will be politely shown the door.'

'Well, I still think it's a little cruel to string people along.'

Molly gave a sad smile. 'Which of us hasn't done it at some time or another? All of us need to feel loved and wanted. Why should Chester prove the exception? His money and power don't make him impervious to basic human needs, in fact the very opposite. And speaking of basic human needs,' Molly put down her empty cup and stretched her spine, 'I'm just about ready for a small nap!'

Kate sat for a while, deep in her thoughts. Loving parents and a happy childhood had supplied her with a surfeit of emotional security and unlike her childhood friends, for whom excitement lay in the smell of orange blossom and a diamond solitaire on their third finger, excitement for Kate lay in the unknown, the unfamiliar. Security and certitude were states she found dull and drear. But what happens when the reserves—when time—begins to run out? Wide-eyed expectancy, like youthful exuberance, begins to look a little contrived in older women. She thought of Joanna, with Simon. Of Molly, with money and status. Which of the two would be the happier in ten years' time? Which of them had made the right choice? Liberation had provided women with opportunity and choice, but left *them* to make the decision. It was not the becoming, but the being free that brought the problems.

Outside the evening was closing in, and Kate uncurled herself lazily from the soft chair. She switched on a table light and studied her face dispassionately in a large blemished mirror on the wall; not liking what she saw, she made a face and wandered through to the adjoining bathroom. After the day's bustle, bed seemed a much better prospect than a social evening with Chester Jones and company, but then she remembered Alain Boivin's promise to dine with them. Perhaps the evening might not be as dull as she feared.

After soaking in a warm bath, Kate's spirits lifted and she suddenly felt in the mood to enjoy herself. As she closed the balcony windows in her bedroom, the small courtyard below was humming with the din of conversation, guests were beginning to appear on their way to dinner, full of the day's events. From the dining room across the way there was the discreet sound of china and cutlery. A feeling of anticipation seemed to hang in the air.

Although she had reservations over Chester Jones' presence, Alain's intention to appear that evening encouraged Kate to take pains with her appearance, and she was pleased she had brought along her favourite top, a pink satin camisole. Its colour went splendidly with her black suit, as well as complementing the warm honey tone of her skin, and its thin straps fell delicately across her smooth shoulders. About her neck, a single strand of seed pearls perfectly matched the small pearl buttons down the front of the camisole. Finally she slipped into a pair of black evening sandals and took a last look in the mirror. Her hair fell smoothly upon her shoulders, its highlights softly gleaming in the pool of light, and this time she did not make a face.

Throwing her jacket about her shoulders, she joined Molly and the rest of the buyers in the foyer of the hotel, and in an elated mood they made their way in several taxis to Montmartre. The taxis deposited them in a narrow cobbled street, outside a small restaurant that emitted muffled sounds of people enjoying themselves. The others entered the premises with a smiling familiarity; Kate followed with a slight feeling of trepidation in the pit of her stomach.

The restaurant was divided into several rooms. In the first was a long bar and lots of noisy good humour; a sea of bodies moved in time to drink and the music of an old man playing an accordion. Molly managed to exchange a few words with one of the waiters, who led them through a door and into the restaurant proper, a large room at the rear of the premises. A long central table had been reserved for their party and as they settled themselves in their seats, they all declared themselves starving.

Kate's eyes took a while to grow accustomed to the low lighting and it was Molly who pointed out the three newcomers—Chester Jones, Alain Boivin and Erika Gibbs.

'Just like her,' sniffed Molly, 'getting herself invited to our treat.'

'I don't suppose she had to try very hard in that outfit,' replied Kate. The emerald green dress followed every line and curve of Erika's figure as well as complementing her fine white skin. The severe topknot had disappeared and long auburn hair now fell heavily about her face.

Molly nudged Kate in the ribs. 'Is that cleavage intentional or a terrible accident?'

Kate giggled into her glass. 'You have to admit, she certainly knows how to make an entrance.'

'So does Miss Piggy.'

Perhaps it was something of a bravura performance, thought Kate as she watched Erika glide like visiting royalty across the room, fully aware of herself and her effect, but Kate had also seen the male glances she had collected on the way. Ahead of her Alain strode up the room to join them, throwing open his arms. 'So many beautiful women! And in one evening!'

Beckoning over a waiter, he ordered some aperitifs, then pulled up a chair beside Kate, his eyes complimenting her appearance. It was a look she had grown accustomed to over the years, but on the right occasion, never failed to please. Once the drinks had arrived, he proceeded to entertain them with an account of his recent attempt to mediate between a German buyer and a Korean manufacturer, each convinced of the other's dishonesty.

'Neither spoke each other's language, and French only poorly,' he added.

'What did you do?' asked Kate.

He shrugged a shoulder. 'Raised my fee, of course!'

Kate found it easy to join in the laughter and caught herself smiling in Chester Jones' direction as he approached their table.

'Chester—at last!' called out Molly. 'Don't you know it's very bad form in these days of equality to keep your staff waiting for their food?'

He smiled apologies around the table. 'I'm sorry, I had to make a phone call to Milan and I had problems getting through.'

Molly waved her glass. 'No excuses—and especially, no business! Your older employees require sustenance.'

He picked up a menu. 'What have you all chosen?' He smiled across at Kate, who suddenly felt she might be at the beginning of a very pleasant evening.

The food decided upon and ordered, there was about the occasion an air almost of festivity, as laughter and wine flowed up and down the table. Although the tables were somewhat cramped, the decor was informal and delightfully intimate, with flickering candles and warm red walls. Tantalising smells drifted across from the kitchen that stood in full view of the tables and added to the atmosphere of the place. The waiters smiled easily, actually appearing to enjoy their work, and soon were producing an assortment of mouthwatering dishes. Portions were plentiful and lots of hot garlic bread and good wine added to the enjoyment.

The restaurant was a family affair, whose reputation for delicious, simple French cooking had been handed down from generation to generation and zealously guarded by each custodian. Even the occasional shout from a harassed chef to one of his underlings only added to the family spirit, and judging by the crush, their formula for good food and friendly surroundings was a successful one.

'Why is it that French food always looks as good as it tastes,' simpered Erika, 'while in English restaurants it's the other way around; it tastes as bad as it looks!'

Alain smiled. 'In France, we like our food the way we like our women . . . pleasing to the eye.'

Erika smiled provocatively back at him across her wine glass. 'That doesn't say much for English women.'

'Or English cabbage, for that matter,' observed Molly, breaking the spell Erika was hoping to cast, but Alain had already turned away to address a remark to Chester. Erika, nonplussed, sipped her wine and looked across at Kate.

'Is this your first visit to Paris?' she asked.

'I came earlier this year.'

Erika raised an eyebrow. 'What a lot of travelling you do on Christopher's behalf. I'm quite impressed. I thought only buyers justified the expense.' She smiled as she spoke and the hint of malice in her observation was scarcely discernible.

'If that were so,' interjected Molly, sensing Kate's unease, 'then *your* presence over the years must take some explaining.'

A look of instinctive hostility flashed between the two women.

'That wasn't what I meant.'

'Whatever you meant,' interrupted Chester, 'don't you think we've all had enough shop talk for today, Erika?'

Not waiting for or expecting a reply, Chester Jones immediately turned his attention back to Alain. Kate felt somewhat bemused by the incident; the man had been deep in conversation, yet had apparently heard theirs. Hadn't he once told her that nothing escaped him? However, nothing had appeared to bother Erika, who was now chatting away vivaciously to her other neighbour.

Alain leant across and refilled Kate's glass. 'You are very young to have so much responsibility,' he commented.

'I'm really here under false pretences,' she explained. 'My boss couldn't make it at the last moment.'

'Whatever the reason . . .' He raised his glass in a silent toast. 'How long do you plan to stay?'

'Two more days.'

He grimaced, then smiled engagingly. 'I am coming to London soon, perhaps we could meet then?'

Kate smiled her acquiescence. He was an attractive man, she knew she looked attractive, and the dangerous combination of good wine and Gallic charm was beginning to take its pleasurable effect. Soon they were chatting away like old friends. Once or twice she glanced across at Chester Jones, but he was engrossed in a lively debate with several of the buyers. Later, as the waiters began clearing away the empty dishes, he requested the bill and after discreetly settling the account, pushed back his chair and got purposefully to his feet. 'Chester, you can't run out on us now!' admonished Molly. 'Alain has promised to take us to see a notorious floor show.'

He smiled apologetically. 'I've an early flight to Milan in the morning, but don't change your plans on my account.'

'Won't you stay and have some coffee, at least?' pleaded Molly, but he shook his head.

As he had been speaking Erika had gathered her stole about her and now stood beside him, smiling her farewells, his earlier rebuttal either forgotten or forgiven.

'She looks as if she's just won him in a raffle,' whispered Molly, looking after the departing couple with a thoughtful expression. 'When the time comes, that little lady will be none too pleased at having to step down.'

'Maybe she won't have to. She's an attractive woman and he doesn't appear to dislike her company,' observed Kate.

'He's too much of a gentleman to let it appear otherwise.' Molly lit up a cigarette. 'One thing I'm sure of, joining us for dinner and leaving with him this evening was of her own making.'

'Both of which she did with style,' smiled Kate. 'There wasn't a man in the room who didn't catch her arrival.'

'Making headlines is her business,' grunted Molly. 'Easily seen, easily forgotten.'

Kate frowned. 'I'm not so sure. After all, it takes more than a pretty face to hold down the kind of job she does.'

'Oh, she's clever all right—at making friends in the right places. If it suited her purpose she'd chew you to bits!'

'Why should Chester Jones be involved with someone like that?' mused Kate.

'If you ask me I don't think he knows he is involved. I told you, she's a clever woman. She's managed to get most things she wanted, only now it's Chester.'

'You think then that he might marry her?'

'I said he was a gentleman,' said Molly. 'I didn't say his brain was softening.'

As they lingered over coffee somebody suggested it was time they went on to another club, but a generous supply of black coffee had had a sobering effect on Kate and she pleaded fatigue. Arrangements were made to take her back to the hotel first and, in spite of gentle persuasion from Alain to do otherwise, she alighted at the corner of the Rue de Faubourg-St Honoré and waved her goodbyes. After the day's sunshine there was a chill in the air that made her shiver, and she hugged her jacket about her as she walked the short distance to the hotel.

Pleased to be back in her warm room, Kate slipped off her jacket and reached for the light switch, decided otherwise and walked languidly across to the french windows. She drew back the curtains and looked out. Several latecomers were sauntering across the courtyard, their conversation drifting up, then away. In the unlit room, lights from the courtyard lamps cast shadows on to the ceiling. It had, after all, been an enjoyable evening and Kate wondered if she had made the right decision not to go along with the others. The heat of the room felt suddenly oppressive and she lifted up her hair from the back of her neck and laid her cheek against the cool pane of glass. Her lips curved into a secret smile as she thought of the evening's events.

'May I share the joke?'

She looked up startled as a yellow pool of light suddenly lit up the room and revealed the seated figure of a man. Kate stared back at Chester Jones, too stunned to speak.

'I'm sorry if I frightened you.'

'What on earth are you doing here?' she exclaimed, letting her hair spill back on to her bare shoulders.

'I'm paying the bill. What's your excuse?'

Her thoughts became confused, and then she remembered the arrangements made for him to share the suite. She flushed a little and bit her lip.

'You startled me,' she said, not knowing if it was anger she felt or relief. 'I thought it was only bogeymen you met in the dark.'

'You believe in bogeymen?'

'I didn't, but now I'm not so sure.' She returned his smile. 'You do have a habit of popping out of the woodwork!'

He waited a moment, watching her in a considering way, then said: 'I don't appear to have made much of an impression on you so far.'

'I wouldn't go so far as to say that ... In fact, quite the opposite.'

'I suppose recent events haven't shown me in much of a good light, what with Joanna growing up overnight,' he agreed.

'One of the annoying habits children have, growing up.'

'I know, it happens in the best of families. I only wish, for her sake, the transformation had been less painful.'

'Sometimes the child needs to break away from her family in order to be treated as an adult,' Kate reminded him.

He lay back in his chair and took a long, slow look at her face. 'I hadn't expected anyone back here so soon. Why aren't you with the others?'

'Exhaustion caught up with me.'

His face creased into a smile. 'Ah yes, now I remember, your dislike of public occasions ...'

She returned his smile. 'This evening I enjoyed myself immensely. The food, the wine and the company ... everything was perfect.'

'Of course, the company ...' A tone had crept into his voice. 'Tell me, Miss Whelan, how did you find Monsieur Boivin?'

'I found him ... charming company.'

'Mm ...' he mused.

'What's that supposed to mean?'

'I'm simply agreeing—that you did appear to enjoy his company.'

Kate blushed at the insinuation behind his words and responded defensively. 'How right you are! He's charming, he's considerate, and what's more, he actually appears to *like* the female of the species!'

There was a moment's silence. 'Just so long as company policy hasn't slipped your memory, Miss Whelan.'

She stared at him in fury. 'What do you mean?'

'Company policy disapproves of fraternisation between employees. I believe I've mentioned that to you once before.'

'How dare you! How dare you presume . . .' She bristled with hostility and then, in spite of herself, her eyes suddenly filled with tears. 'Why do you take so much pleasure in goading me?' She shook her head in frustration. 'You must hate me so much.'

He rose abruptly to his feet and came and stood by her. 'Forgive me . . . Please don't cry.' He spoke in a low, gentle voice and held her until she calmed.

Exhausted by the late hour and their emotional exchange, Kate made no attempt to resist the comforting gesture, but instead lay trembling against his chest, distantly conscious of his arm about her waist, his hand gently stroking her hair. He waited until her tears had subsided then pushed her slightly away, the better to see her. When she looked up at him, his eyes were showing concern.

'I really didn't intend to upset you,' he said gently. 'I feel awful.'

She smiled and her hands went to her tear-stained face. 'And I probably look awful!'

'No, Kate, no . . . you don't look awful.' He spoke slowly and deliberately, his dark eyes grown suddenly intent, wrapped in his thoughts and the shadows. Once again he was the elusive stranger. Nothing had really changed, thought Kate, strangely disappointed, and yet there were still his hands upon her arms, tracing the shape of her bare shoulders . . .

In the past his abrasive personality had infuriated her, but now this sudden show of concern for her feelings had revealed a warmth in him she had never suspected, and its effect was all the more disturbing. The noise of a distant car engine broke into the silence and reluctantly she drew away.

'I'm sorry . . . I don't know what came over me.'

Chester spoke soothingly. 'It's been a long day. We're both tired.'

'People like you aren't supposed to get tired,' smiled Kate, attempting to lighten the mood that had descended upon them both.

He grinned. 'You think it might worry the share-holders if they got to hear about it?'

'Doesn't it worry Erika?'

'Erika?' His eyebrows shot up. 'Why should it?'

She shrugged a shoulder. 'I thought you and she would be enjoying the night life of Paris.'

'Erika possibly is, but my appetites are simpler. I prefer a less hectic life-style.'

'She doesn't mind? Your not escorting her, I mean?'

He looked puzzled. 'Who am I to spoil her fun? She leads her life, I lead mine.'

'But I thought you and she . . . What I mean is . . .'

He smiled and placed a finger upon her lips. 'Didn't you once warn me against gossip? Erika is simply an old friend. Since we're in the same line of business our paths cross frequently. We might lunch out occasionally to discuss business . . . nothing more.'

He appeared to believe what he said, yet Kate could not help remembering Joanna's remarks on Erika's ulti-mate intentions towards her brother, and Molly's wry comments over dinner. Certainly the familiar manner Erika adopted towards him was not that of a business acquaintance.

'Besides,' he continued, 'she has little need of my company. There's always someone she knows, sporting enough to perform the necessary social duties, even in France.'

'She's certainly an attractive woman,' Kate agreed.

'She knows how to make men think so, which is an-other matter.' He put out a hand and gently ruffled Kate's hair. 'Tell me, what's a nice girl like you doing in a business like this?'

'Trying to make a living.'

'Girls who look like you don't usually have to try. They get locked away in an ivory tower, whiling away the time until a handsome prince happens by.' He spoke more quietly. 'Maybe he has already?'

She shook her head, smiling. 'That only happens in fairy stories.'

'You do have golden hair,' he pointed out.

'But I'm no princess, simply Kate Whelan, late of the sportswear department. You must take me as you find me, Mr Jones.'

'And you,' Mr Jones said slowly, cupping her face in his hands, 'I find adorable.'

'Please,' she whispered, 'don't play games with me.'

'I never play games, Kate.'

He spoke intently and in a moment had taken her in his arms and kissed her. So unexpected was his embrace that at first Kate made no move to stop him, and then she tried to push him away, her senses uncomfortably stirred by the desire she felt in his taut body. But as if paralysed by his touch, she ceased struggling and succumbed to a kiss so intense and demanding that a shudder went down her spine and she lay breathless and silent in his arms.

He tilted her head upwards and sought her eyes, searching for a response. What he saw there only strengthened his desire, for he caught her to him again, and soon she was blissfully drowning beneath his gentle caresses, his tenderness and control tantalising her senses, exciting her beyond endurance until her whole body trembled violently against his and her mouth parted eagerly to receive his kiss.

Under his coaxing her body had come alive with a longing she had never known, and now she submitted pleasurably as his hands explored the soft curves of her body, wanting him to go on for ever . . . powerless to refuse. She offered no resistance as he undid the buttons of her camisole and slid his hands inside, her breasts swelling to his touch. Her breath came faster as he stroked and caressed her, charging her body with such excitement that she cried out beneath his embrace.

There had been excitement and physical attraction in her life, but never had she experienced such ecstasy. Never had another man aroused so much passion in her. It was as if an avalanche of desire had swept away her reasoning faculties, so willing was she to surrender totally, so powerful were the senses he had awakened.

She trembled as he held her close, feeling his hard body press into hers, his hands travelling passionately along the curve of her back, his tongue exploring the smooth line of her shoulders, and then when his mouth came down upon her soft, eager lips a wave of intense pleasure washed over her as she yielded to his kisses; their burning intimacy lifting her to ecstatic heights, as if time itself was suspended . . . and finally gasping for breath, her limbs weak with desire.

His shirt hung loose as she lay limp in his arms, her cheek against his damp skin, her fingers fondling his tousled hair.

'Kate . . . Kate . . .'

She turned her face up to him, her eyes shining, and he gently kissed her forehead. 'I hadn't intended this, but I'm glad it happened. The strain was becoming unbearable.'

'I'm glad it happened too,' she whispered, 'despite this being a *business* trip.'

'I'll book us another room,' he murmured into the warmth of her neck. 'Another hotel, if you prefer.'

As she caught his meaning her body tensed. 'No, Chester . . . No!'

'You can't doubt how I feel about you, Kate?'

His voice made doubt impossible, but still she drew away from him and moved to the window. 'Please, give me time, Chester. Give me time to get used to the idea

. . . What's between us is too precious to spoil too soon.'

'My darling Kate, continue to wear your badge of respectability if you will.' He came and stood behind her, kissing the back of her neck. 'From the moment you walked into my office I've wanted you, but what matters more is what *you* want . . . Love has to be freely given.'

For a long moment they stood in silence and then she turned and looked up. His eyes were filled with longing, and suddenly all that mattered was to feel his arms tightening about her, crushing her against his warm, alive body until she gasped for breath. Powerless to resist the inevitable, she threw her arms about his strong, thick neck, feeling him shudder with emotion at her touch. There was no need for words as her body let him know how much he was wanted, her earlier refusal forgotten, but not by him, for he gently disengaged her hands and held her at arm's length.

'My darling Kate . . . don't make it harder for me.'

As she stood before him his eyes drifted admiringly over her curvaceous figure; her firm swollen breasts, her small neat waist. He reached out and stroked the pale gold of her skin and she had never felt so beautiful.

'To think I came so close to losing this . . . losing you . . .' He bent down and kissed her; a slow intimate kiss that made her tremble with pleasure, then gently he buttoned her top, his face serious. 'Don't make me wait too long, Kate . . . I'm only human.'

She smiled back. 'Not my long-awaited prince? Shame on you, I wouldn't have let you in otherwise!'

'Let me in?' he queried.

'My ivory tower.'

'No lock would ever have kept me out,' he assured her.

'Not even company policy?'

'Now what are you talking about?'

'No fraternisation between employees, Miss Whelan,'

mimicked Kate. 'I believe I mentioned it to you once before.'

He laughed out loud. 'It's my prerogative to break the rules, seeing I made them . . . Besides, I didn't want you falling under some other man's spell.'

'Who says I'm under yours?'

'I do—any objections?' He pulled her against him and she smiled up at him, deliriously happy.

'None at all.'

Chester glanced at his wristwatch. 'It's getting late and you need to sleep.' A smile hovered about his mouth. 'I'll put temptation out of your way, Miss Whelan, and grab a nightcap in the bar downstairs. I can be sure that won't keep me awake!' His eyes grew serious as he cupped his hands about her face. 'Sweet dreams, my darling Kate.' He kissed her gently good-night and for a long moment she remained standing in the middle of the room after he had left, numbed and disbelieving.

Later, in the bedroom, as her clothes slipped to the floor, she caught her reflection in the triple mirror. There was still a look of innocence about her fair hair and dewy complexion, but a man's passion had left her lips red and bruised and there was no mistaking the transformation of the girl into the sensuous woman.

She lay across her bed and wondered at her own incredulity. She hardly knew the man, he was practically a stranger, and yet he had changed her whole life. She thought of their past confrontations, how even this evening he had goaded her with cruel indifference. And yet minutes later, he had held her in his arms and kissed her with a fervour that left her in no doubt as to his feelings, while she in turn had felt her body respond to his as if the bitter past had never been. Her face shone at the memory of Chester and his devil-like powers to arouse in her such primitive passion. What had happened, had happened without any warning, but she knew there would be no regrets with the dawn. What had happened had happened because she had chosen.

She hugged herself and laughed aloud. She had never been so happy. Too restless for sleep, she slipped a light robe about her shoulders and stood at the balcony, her face to the sky. She caught her breath as the chill night air touched her warm flesh and she drew the wrap across her breasts. As she leaned against the narrow parapet she thought of Chester and the response her nearness had aroused in him, and never had she felt so elated in her whole life. His desire for her had shown in every gesture, in every look. And how much she had wanted him! Questions she had never seriously considered before were running through her head, demanding some sort of an answer. What was it he had said? 'Love freely given'? Kate sighed deeply. It was something she would have to come to terms with eventually, but whatever her decision their lives appeared to be fatefully intertwined.

Suddenly she felt an immense fatigue and this time climbed willingly into bed, but as she lay in the dark Chester's image persisted. How ironic was their situation! His enmity had once brought her to the edge of despair, but tonight his love had filled her with exquisite bliss. She wondered what it was that had drawn them together, what mystical force had brought about the improbable. But as her body tensed with longing, she knew full well the answer. She was passionately and deeply in love with Chester Jones.

She smiled to herself, picturing Joanna's reaction. The man who had inflamed her senses tonight, who had suddenly made everything meaningful and worthwhile, was a million miles removed from Joanna's belligerent brother—but then Molly's interpretation of the man had been more revealing. At an age when other men were shrugging off school blazers and conquering strange new worlds, the rough mantle of responsibility had fallen heavily upon Chester's shoulders. With the sudden death

of both parents, he had been compelled to adopt a
father's role before he himself had become a man, and
he had sacrificed too much for too long for Joanna's
happiness to remain unconcerned when Simon Forrest
came upon the scene.

All the more reason, perhaps, not to increase his
burden further with her own expectations. For the first
time in his life, now that Joanna had departed, he would
be free to enjoy the good life as only a wealthy and
footloose bachelor is able, and it would be naïve of Kate
to expect him to think in terms of marriage and domestic
bliss. Her common sense told her that if there was to be
any future between them, it would inevitably be without
the prospect of marriage, but her heart was past caring.
Without knowing it, she had lived her life in anticipation
of a man and a moment, and tonight she would not
think beyond that moment, would ask no commitment
of the man.

CHAPTER NINE

KATE awoke the next day to the smell of steaming black coffee and Molly's casual announcement that Chester had already left for Milan.

'So soon?' said Kate, in a voice that was surprisingly steady.

'Probably to escape Erika, only someone should tell him the world isn't that big,' observed Molly as she handed Kate a cup of coffee. 'I thought you'd be more delighted at the news?'

'Oh, yes, yes ·I am,' insisted Kate, taking the coffee and resting her back against the headboard, 'but he turned out to be such pleasant company, last night.'

'He was, what little time he was there. Businessmen, like time and tide, wait for no man.'

Nor any woman, thought Kate wistfully. At first, she had felt a chill of apprehension on hearing Molly's news, but then she recalled Chester's conversation over dinner the previous evening and his plans to fly to Milan the following morning. After all, he was a businessman—a successful one—and it was inevitable that business should intervene, and on reflection she welcomed the distance that was between them both that morning. She was a little fearful of what daylight might have revealed, and his absence at least gave her two more days of happy illusion.

For the remainder of their Paris trip, work absorbed all Kate's energy. Expeditions, to crowded department stores and far-flung boutiques, were carried out under Molly's brisk supervision and crammed full the daylight hours. And at night exhaustion and sleep did the rest.

With little or no time for recriminations her good

spirits lasted until she returned home, but then the days passed without word from Chester. Why didn't he ring? Surely he must know she was waiting. She had been flattered by the attentions of such a man and no doubt she had indulged *his* ego a little, but was she foolish to think their little flirtation meant anything, to suppose she was more than just another romantic encounter? Perhaps for him it was already at an end, a momentary pleasure, whereas she had made the mistake of letting her heart become involved and now felt thoroughly miserable.

Full of passionate entreaties, he had made no promises, no mention of a future, and yet he had expected Kate to commit herself physically to him! What if she hadn't refused? What if she had spent the night with him? How much greater would her disillusionment have been. Or might she have aroused something deeper in him; the nature of that something forever elusive that binds two people together.

That Friday the flat appeared particularly gloomy and oppressive, and wearying of the waiting, she decided to spend the weekend with married friends in Cambridge. Long walks with their three children and two large dogs provided her with plenty of fresh air and a dose of wholesome reality.

Caught up in their bustling family life, Kate found it easy to rid herself of the despairing mood that had engulfed her all week. Only in the evening after dinner, when the children were asleep in their bedrooms, and the grown-ups had settled themselves in front of the fire with a drink, did she experience a sense of aloneness. She thought about the men in her past who had offered her the security and companionship of marriage and a family, but in particular she thought of Chester; the one man who might have made some sense of her life, but who hadn't offered . . . However much she tried to erase him from her mind Chester's image came back with blinding clarity, and the memory of him tortured her.

A grey Monday morning brought a cheerful phone call from Joanna.

'I've heaps to tell you. So much has happened since we last met!'

Since we last met, Kate felt like saying, I've almost lost an arm and a leg on your account, but instead she allowed Joanna to continue. 'I was hoping you'd put in a good word with Chester for me.'

At this moment in Kate's life, further involvement between Joanna and her brother was just about the last thing she expected or wanted.

'I threw over my job a week ago and don't want him to hear about it on the grapevine.'

'Can't you tell him yourself?'

'I haven't had a chance. He's been away all week, hopping across Europe. I'm going to call him now, but I wanted some friendly support at this end when he erupts. Please say you will.'

Kate felt her spirits soar at Joanna's revelation. That explained why Chester had not contacted her since their Paris trip. He had been out of the country. Not trusting herself to enquire casually about the office as to his whereabouts, she had simply presumed him to be back in London. So there was still a chance . . . Or was there? A week had passed since their encounter. Time for him to consider the possible complications of a romantic dalliance with a member of his staff. Time enough to develop immunity.

'Would you?' urged Joanna.

'I'm sorry?' queried Kate.

'My job. Be a pet and back me up.'

'From where I stand you appear more than capable of dealing with any opposition from your brother,' Kate said dryly.

'That might be your impression, Kate, but all this squabbling is getting me down.'

'He's certain to come round in time. To see things your way.'

'I'm not so sure. He still refuses to see Simon.'

'You make him sound like the villain in some third-rate soap opera,' laughed Kate, her happiness beginning to bubble over. 'I have visions of him threatening Simon with a shotgun and ordering him never to darken his threshold again.'

'It's not funny, Kate, Chester is my brother and I love him dearly, but he's driving me away, forcing me to make a choice . . . and in the end I'll choose Simon.'

'You're right, it isn't funny,' said Kate, regretting her flippant remarks, 'and I promise that if the occasion arises I'll do my best PR job on your behalf.'

As she returned to Monday's workload, Kate's air of emelancholy had visibly receded, and she moved about the office with the breezy concern of a woman totally committed to the trivia of office administration. Chester's was the fourth phone call that morning.

'Kate?' There was no mistaking that voice, and her heart leapt. 'Did you hear about Joanna?'

'Her resignation, you mean? Yes, she rang me this morning.'

'Her resignation, hell! She was given the sack.'

Kate flinched at his brusque tone. 'What for?'

'Punctuality—or rather her lack of it. She's forever going on about her independence, being responsible for her own future. She can't even get herself out of bed in the morning.'

'It's quite a journey to the airport from where she's living,' Kate pointed out.

'Then she ought to have considered that beforehand. It's what being adult and responsible is all about.'

'She's adult enough to want to end this childish squabbling,' said Kate tightly.

'Not *quite* adult enough . . . As I'm her guardian, my

signature is still required on a legal document—something to do with this legacy, and she was ringing to jolt my memory. I have it here and I was hoping you'd deliver it for me. After our set-to on the telephone, I'm not her most favourite postman. Would you mind coming up to my office?'

She had wanted so much to see him. Throughout the days she had waited and the waiting had been unbearable, but now her moment of joy on hearing his voice had long gone. She spoke calmly, despite the betrayal she felt.

'If you don't mind, I'd rather not get involved.'

He did not answer at once, but when he did there was a quiet intensity in his voice.

'Please, Kate . . . please!'

She continued for a moment to hold the phone to her ear, then slowly lowered the receiver.

Chester was seated at his desk absorbed in thought when Miss Johnson ushered Kate into his office, but the scowl on his face disappeared when he looked up and saw her.

'Thank you for coming,' he said, as the door closed behind her.

She shrugged. 'You pay my wages.'

He rubbed his cheek and smiled for the first time. 'I'm sorry I lost my temper. I've not been getting much sleep lately.'

'Business or pleasure?' asked Kate sarcastically.

'Crowded airports and delayed flights. Never my idea of a pleasant time.'

'Perhaps that's what Joanna thought and why she resigned.'

'Having to deal with disgruntled passengers like me, you mean?' He shook his head. 'Maybe you're right. Maybe I shouldn't have flown off the handle quite so fast—but then Joanna just seems to have that effect.'

'Like me, you mean?'

'You? Oh, yes, you have an effect, Kate.' He came a pace nearer and her stomach knotted. 'I tried to call you yesterday . . . and the night before.'

'I was away,' she told him.

'Business or pleasure?'

'It was meant to be pleasurable . . .' She lowered her eyes as he moved closer, full of the memory of their last meeting.

'And . . .?' he prompted.

She could smell his fragrance now and her longing for him was intense. 'I've not been getting much sleep either.'

He put out his hand and lightly touched her cheek. 'I thought you might have given me up as a bad job?'

Kate smiled back at him and slowly shook her head. She had waited so long, but now he was with her and the more touch of his hand had dispelled her terrible doubts.

Her skin tingled as he gently traced the soft curves of her cheek and throat. 'You're a woman of disturbing contradictions, Kate, with your look of childlike innocence.'

She smiled mischievously. 'Don't let it distract you from the rest of me!'

His hands travelled slowly down to her waist. 'Everything about you is distracting, my dearest Kate.'

He pulled her firmly into his arms and as their bodies touched she could feel the certainty of his desire and knew that nothing had changed. And so she clung to him and responded passionately to his kisses, no longer afraid to show her true feelings.

'Kate!' He pushed her gently away, his face pale and perspiring. 'Don't you know you could seduce a man like that?'

'That's what I was hoping,' she teased, parting her mouth persuasively.

He pulled her to him and she felt his breath warm

against her throat, his hard body pressed against hers. 'Who's arguing?' he whispered hoarsely in her ear. And then her arms tightened about his neck as time and again she yielded to the force of his kisses, kisses that filled her with an exquisite bliss. After a long moment they drew apart and still with his arm about her Chester stretched out towards his desk intercom and pressed a button.

'Hold all my calls, please.'

'What on earth will your secretary think?' whispered Kate.

'She's paid extremely well not to think—out loud, that is. That was the switchboard—I told Miss Johnson to go to lunch once you appeared.'

'You were that certain I'd come?'

He nuzzled her neck. 'I wasn't ... but you're here now, and that's all that matters.'

For the first time she noticed the dark shadows about his eyes and she felt a wave of tenderness.

'You look tired. Let me get you a drink.'

He sank into a chair and watched her pleasurably as she moved towards the bar in the corner of the room. When she had poured his drink he patted the seat beside him.

'Come and sit next to me.'

He lay back in his chair gazing at the ceiling and she was content simply to be near him, to share their growing intimacy.

'You work too hard,' Kate murmured, gently stroking his forehead with her fingers.

Chester smiled expansively. 'Don't blame work, Kate.' He stretched out a hand and laid it in her lap. 'It's you that drains my energies.'

Her skin tingled at his touch and she felt herself blush.

'I can see that matters will have to be resolved soon,' he teased.

'I hope that doesn't mean another transfer?'

He laughed out loud. 'My darling Kate, if it didn't work the first time why should it now?'

'I don't understand?'

'Doing business with you became something of an occupational hazard; the more angry you became, the more beautiful you appeared, and as director of buying I couldn't afford to have my judgment swayed by such feminine wiles.'

'Feminine wiles! Feminine wiles!' Kate sat forward abruptly in her seat.

'What are you talking about? You behaved abominably and I *hated* you!'

'And now?' He took her hand in his and pressed it to his mouth.

'You haven't been out of my thoughts,' she whispered, and as she spoke she realised it was the simple truth.

Chester looked at his wristwatch. 'Have you made any plans for lunch?'

She shook her head.

'Good. You can have it with me.'

'As long as I don't end up being the main course!'

He leant across and rubbed the tip of his tongue along her ear. 'I'll save you for dessert.'

She laughed and gently pushed him away. 'What if your secretary should come in?'

'That didn't deter you a moment ago,' he teased, smoothing back her hair. 'If it worries you I could make other arrangements.'

'It's the *other arrangements* that worry me,' she smiled, wrinkling her nose provocatively.

'You need have no worries on my account, Miss Whelan. I guarantee customer satisfaction.'

In spite of her blush, she giggled happily at his teasing insinuation.

He picked up the telephone and ordered some lunch. When he had replaced the receiver, he considered a

moment, then reached into his inside jacket pocket.
'Here.' He took her hand and gently closed her fingers
around a small package. Kate looked puzzled. 'Go
ahead, it's yours,' he said, watching her unwrap a small
gold medallion—a medallion she had worn constantly
on the chain about her neck, until one morning she had
found it missing. 'You dropped it in my office the first
day we met,' he told her. The link appeared to have
broken.'

'You've had it all this time?'

'I don't need it now . . .'

Her heart swelled up. She wanted to throw her arms
about him, tell him how much she loved him, but a
knock on the door announced the arrival of lunch and
the words were left unsaid.

Lunch was a simple affair: a selection of cold meats
with slices of fresh rye bread, a large bowl of mixed
salad, generous portions of Stilton, and to finish, a
basket of small tangerines. Faced with this appetising
spread, Kate suddenly realised how hungry she was. She
smiled contentedly across at Chester as he proceeded to
open a bottle of wine. 'Is this your usual fare?'

He released the cork and filled her glass. 'It's not every
day I entertain a beautiful woman.'

'I thought men in your position were deluged with
luncheon invitations.'

'Men in my position usually haven't the time. We have
to work hard to maintain our position, which means *not*
accepting luncheon invitations.'

'Not even those from beautiful young women?' Kate
smiled at him over the rim of her glass.

'My invitations are usually from plain and elderly
businessmen, although I suppose some of them might
think they're young and beautiful! Anyway, why should
I bother when I have beautiful employees?'

He smiled across at her and raised his glass, but Kate's
face had grown suddenly serious. 'Is that my fascination,

Chester? Someone to pass the office hours, lighten the workaday doldrums?'

He did not answer immediately. 'I had hoped that's all it might be. After all, resisting the physical charms of my staff has become something of a way of life, but with you . . .' He shook his head, then drained his glass. 'I just don't seem to have any choice.'

'I'd suspect that was a compliment if only you didn't sound so gloomy about it,' laughed Kate.

'I'm responsible for the largest retailing consortium in the country. I pass daily judgment on a turnover worth millions . . . then you appear and I'm floundering! A simple human situation and I can't handle it.' He raised the flat of his free hand and smiled. 'And you wonder why I sound so gloomy?'

As she joined in his laughter, Kate thought of their first meeting, when he had lost his temper with her in that very office and the bitterness she had felt at his subsequent behaviour. Now it was enough just for him to be there for her happiness to be complete.

When they had eaten Chester pushed away his empty coffee cup and lit a small cigar. 'Will you see Joanna for me?'

She hesitated. 'Do I have to?'

'No, of course you don't have to. I'd just feel a lot happier if you did. Perhaps you could talk some sense into her.'

'I don't think she'd pay much attention to anything I might have to say.'

'If only she didn't think of Forrest as her intrepid knight in shining armour!' he sighed.

'And if you didn't insist he'd just crawled out from under a stone.'

'Joanna's opinion is based on youthful delusion, mine on fact.'

'You sound pretty certain of your case,' Kate commented.

'I am,' he said emphatically. 'Certain that soon she'll be faced with all the sordid details.'

'In that case, she'll be more in need of a shoulder to cry on than a mouthful of platitudes.'

'That's one of the reasons I'd like you to be around when it happens,' he said. 'When it happens she's going to have to do a lot of growing up.'

'Isn't that what you wanted?'

'Maybe . . . but I don't like to see her getting hurt.'

'You can't really have one without the other.'

'You're right, of course, but why did it have to be Simon Forrest? Why couldn't she have fallen for some nice solicitor who drives a family saloon, with a paid up road licence, and live peacefully ever after in South Kensington?'

'Nice solicitors with family saloons no longer live in South Kensington, it's full of bedsits.'

'Neasden, then?'

'Because once she'd married and settled down with Mr Nice in Neasden, it wouldn't be long before she was hankering after the likes of Simon Forrest,' Kate assured him. 'Joanna's a romantic, it's important she get's such a man out of her system.'

'I'd like to get him out of my system,' Chester muttered.

'There doesn't appear much likelihood of that; he seems set up for life at the *Dispatch*.'

'Mmm . . .' A strange expression crossed his face. 'As a matter of fact, I'm seeing Adam Sinclair this afternoon.'

Adam Sinclair! The editor of the *Sunday Dispatch*. Kate wondered what business Chester might have with Simon's employer. At her questioning look he started to say something, but changed his mind when the office door opened and the impeccably groomed figure of Erika Gibbs appeared.

'Chester . . . Miss Whelan!' Her smile did not waver

as she strolled languidly across to an empty chair. 'I hope you don't mind my intrusion, but your secretary was out of the office . . .' As she dropped gracefully into the chair her eyes glanced across at the remains of their meal. 'I hope I'm not interrupting anything?'

'We've finished our lunch. Would you like some coffee?'

'I'd prefer something a little stronger. I've just come from an editorial meeting.'

'What was it you wanted to see me about?' asked Chester, pouring her a drink.

Erika crossed her legs and carefully arranged her skirt. 'Actually, it was Miss Whelan I really wanted to see. Publicity said she was with you and I decided to kill two birds with one visit. Have you told Miss Whelan of our plans?'

'Plans?' he queried.

Erika smiled across at Kate. 'He'd forget his own head if I let him! Surely you haven't forgotten, Chester? The publicity campaign for your new department.'

A frown crossed his face. 'I presumed you'd dealt directly with Publicity on that matter, Erika.'

'What was it you had in mind?' asked Kate.

'Bennett's is to run an advertising campaign in several of the dailies to promote their new French department. At the same time the *Gazette* is planning a colour spread on French designers, and I suggested to Chester a possible link-up between us both,' Erika explained.

'If we agree to making our advertising promotion exclusive to the *Gazette*, Erika will guarantee us a full-page editorial in her column, as well as mentions in their colour spread,' explained Chester. 'What do you think, Kate?'

'Sounds like good commercial sense for both parties.'

'I'd especially like to feature some of the outfits bought from the recent collections,' Erika told her.

'Sounds feasible so long as the buyers haven't already

placed their orders,' said Kate. 'An editorial would mean increased demand for a particular style, and stocks might be inadequate.'

'Kate's right,' said Chester, 'with our reputation we can't afford not to have sufficient back-up. You should have agreed things with Christopher last week.'

Erika shrugged an elegant shoulder. 'With so much money involved I naturally thought you'd want the last word.'

'As Head of the Publicity Department Christopher Lloyd has that authority and should have been consulted.'

She stood up and moved closer to Chester, a petulant smile on her lips. 'You know how happier I am dealing with you.'

'Nevertheless, you must concern Christopher in all future negotiations.'

Erika smiled with mock servitude, then turned to Kate. 'Perhaps you could arrange a meeting for me with Christopher for tomorrow morning?'

'Why not this afternoon?' interrupted Chester in a businesslike tone. 'With so much money involved we can't afford to waste any more time.'

Mrs Johnson's sudden appearance in the doorway, announcing Chester's next appointment, brought their discussion to a timely end and Kate rose to leave. Their idyllic moment together had long passed and now, she thought regretfully, Erika's hovering presence would prevent any fond farewells from Chester.

As she walked with Erika along the plush-carpeted corridor Kate checked her wristwatch.

'Christopher should be back from lunch now, and I suggest we bring him up to date before we go any further.'

'I had hoped to choose some styles this afternoon,' protested Erika.

Kate shook her head. 'It makes more sense to begin on paper; outline our basic requirements, then check details of stock with the buyers.'

As they entered the crowded lift, Erika greeted one of the men with a smile of recognition and began talking to him with vivacious affectation. It appeared that both had shared junior status at the same provincial newspaper and had long since gone their separate ways; he to the grey regions of city news, she to the more glamorous section of the media. When they finally emerged on to the third floor Erika turned her attention back to Kate.

'He used to be everybody's dream boy, although you wouldn't think it to look at him now. Two long years we made tea and plans together . . .'

'How long have you been with the *Gazette*?' Kate asked, partly out of curiosity, partly to make conversation.

'Not as long as Chester would have you believe,' said Erika, giving a breathy laugh. 'He's determined to tempt me away one of these days with lots of noughts.'

'He wants you to work for Bennett's?'

'To reorganise Publicity.'

'The Publicity Department?' Kate frowned. 'What about Christopher?'

'It was to be on a consultancy basis . . . at first.' Erika's tone became confidential. 'Chester felt it could do with some shaking up.'

'What stopped you taking up the offer?' Kate asked tightly, wondering where truth left off and fantasy began, and whether Erika herself even knew.

The latter pursed her lips. 'If I were truthful, I suppose I rather enjoy my star billing with the *Gazette*. Of course, I have the occasional blow-up with my editor when he tampers with my copy, but otherwise I'm pretty content with my lot. Besides . . .' she faltered, and cast a sideways glance at Kate, 'Chester has never admired women who are too available.'

'Oh, I wouldn't say that,' smiled Kate, resisting a sudden urge to shake the stupid woman, 'he seems to think very highly of Miss Johnson.'

'That wasn't what I had in mind,' retorted Erika tartly.

'What about his hectic social life? Those numerous girl-friends that supposedly fill his waking hours—and some of the sleeping ones, if we believe everything we're told?' quizzed Kate, determined to break through this ridiculous charade.

'There's no denying that his money and status attract *available* women,' said Erika, ignoring Kate's flippant remarks, 'but he has a way of keeping such affairs low key, if you get my meaning? A man in his position can't afford to become publicly involved with such women . . .'

For the remainder of the afternoon, Kate worked alongside the journalist, applying herself meticulously to their precise tasks, but later, when Erika had left, a bleak mood engulfed her and she found it hard to concentrate on her work. Erika's insinuations had depressed her and now the doubts began gathering strength. Had there been, was there still, something between Chester and Erika? Had Erika spoken the truth, and was Chester's denial of a romantic attachment between himself and Erika mere bluff? It had been easy to lie in his arms and believe otherwise, but now she could not help but wonder . . . Was she simply the latest in a line of other women who had each in her turn succumbed to his charm, and considered of little consequence by Erika who had seen it all before? Was she, Erika, playing a waiting game, quietly confident of her own strong relationship with Chester? The possibility was more than Kate could bear.

That evening as she lay in bed, unable to sleep, her fingers curled around the small medallion hung about her neck. Was it possible that Erika had spoken out of envy and bitterness? Was she fighting for what she believed was rightfully hers ... because that something was slipping surely out of her grasp?

CHAPTER TEN

DESPITE the morning's drizzle, Kate awoke bright-eyed and early the next morning, full of the memory of her reunion with Chester; the tender moments they had shared together in his office and his passionate endearments. Alongside such recollections Erika's gloomy disclosures, Kate decided, were of no account.

'What do you think of my plans for the French promotion?' asked Christopher, seated at his desk hunched over several sheets of paper.

Kate picked up one of the sheets and studied the closely typed lines. 'You must have sat up all night to get this finished.'

'We haven't much time to spare, so I did the rough notes yesterday evening and assembled it all early this morning. I'd like you to read it through and let me have your comments.' He glanced at his wristwatch. 'I need to get copies to each of the buyers and one of the girls can deliver a copy to Erika's office.' He shuffled the papers together. 'It was a good idea of Chester's to involve the *Gazette*—makes economic sense.'

'I got the impression the suggestion came from Erika,' said Kate, wandering across to her own desk.

'You sound as if you disapprove?'

'Of the idea, no.'

He looked over at Kate and gave a conspiratorial wink. 'Don't worry, she only has to choose the styles. I can't imagine her wanting to involve herself in any further headache. Speaking of headaches, I'd like *you* to take responsibility for the whole project.'

'Are you sure? After all, my experience with Publicity is fairly limited . . . I'm not sure I'd be capable of tackling the job singlehanded.'

'Tackling Erika, you really mean?'

'That too.'

'Listen and smile politely, but don't take any nonsense from her and you'll manage perfectly.'

'That shouldn't be too difficult,' said Kate, 'I had practice enough in Paris.'

'Molly was complaining over lunch that she hounded you all on your trip.'

Kate smiled. 'Just some of us some of the time.'

'And Chester all of the time, eh?' He stood up and collected his papers together. 'You've got to admit, she never gives up easily, does our Miss Gibbs.'

'Mm,' murmured Kate, attending to some paper-work.

Not for the first time Kate wondered if the turmoil she felt inside whenever Chester's name was mentioned might be discerned by others. She felt very vulnerable in her present situation; aware that any suspicion of her involvement with one of the directors would inevitably lead to gossip, and office gossip, she knew, was the surest way of ending the affair before it had even begun.

As the morning progressed and she heard nothing from Chester, a sense of depression threatened to over-whelm her and her heart jerked painfully each time the phone rang, although its silence became more agonising than its shrill ring. Unable to settle to anything, Kate decided to take an early lunch on the insistence of Serena Roberts.

'Whoever he is, he isn't worth missing your food over. It's a principle I've always stuck to.'

Kate smiled at her plump colleague. 'Whatever makes you think it's a he?'

'There are only two reasons why women jump when the phone rings ... men; those they want to ring and those they don't.'

When Kate returned from lunch in a more lighthearted mood, it was to find a pale Joanna staring morosely out of the window.

'Joanna!' exclaimed Kate in surprise. 'What are you doing here?'

'I hope you don't mind . . . I had nowhere else to go.'

The distress in her voice was evident and Kate guided the tearful girl towards a chair. The small, pale figure collapsed on to the chair and Kate was reminded of the first evening she and Joanna had met, and the chain of events that had followed.

'Won't you tell me what's wrong?'

Silence, and then the words came out in a breathless tumble. 'Simon has broken off our engagement . . . he's lost his job and gone home to Ireland, and it's all Chester's doing!'

'What has your brother to do with it?' queried Kate.

'He used his friendship with Simon's boss to get Simon fired.'

Kate shook her head in bewilderment. 'I can't believe it.'

'Whether you choose to believe it or not makes little difference,' said Joanna bitterly. 'Simon's gone and he's not coming back.'

'What happened?'

'Sinclair saw Chester yesterday afternoon and that evening Simon was given notice, or rather a month's pay in lieu of notice.'

Despite her concern, Kate remained sceptical about Joanna's accusation. Hadn't she been with Chester the previous day, and hadn't he mentioned seeing Sinclair that afternoon? If he had been planning anything devious, it seemed highly unlikely that he would publicise the event beforehand. No, she refused to believe him capable of such an underhand manoeuvre.

'It's quite an accusation to make against your brother,' she pointed out.

'He hates Simon.'

'I can't believe he'd force him out of his job—and besides, Adam Sinclair isn't a man to dismiss his own employee on anybody's say-so.'

'Chester isn't anybody. He wields a big stick ... He probably threatened to withdraw all his advertising.'

'We don't advertise now in the *Dispatch*,' said Kate, 'and even if we did, can you really imagine your brother stooping so low?'

'Yes, I can and yes, he did,' cried Joanna, whose voice was now bordering on the hysterical. 'Why are you defending him all of a sudden? I suppose he's won you over like all the rest.'

'Nobody has *won* me over, I just want to be sure of the facts. *You* must be sure before confronting him. You could be wrong.'

'I'm not wrong about Simon,' said Joanna, her dark eyes filled with anguish. 'He packed his bags last night and moved out of his flat.'

'But why leave *you*?'

She shrugged. 'His pride, I suppose ... he is a proud man, despite what Chester says. He refuses to live on my money and in Ireland he can be sure of work.'

'Surely there are other jobs in London?' said Kate.

'After that kind of instant dismissal? You know what a gossipy lot journalists are. What newspaper would want to know?'

'I'm certain you're wrong, Joanna. Simon has built up quite a reputation for himself.'

'All the more reason for people to have their suspicions.'

'But a man of his experience must have business contacts, journalist friends who could help him out?'

Joanna shook her head. 'If he has, he never said ... He never really said much at all. It was me who did most of the yelling and screaming. When I discovered he was leaving I just fell to pieces.'

'Perhaps in the cold light of day he may see things a

little differently and regret his action.'

Joanna appeared unconvinced. 'Chester always said he'd do anything to break us up, and he has.'

Suddenly she put her elbows on the desk and buried her face in her hands, and as the tears spilled over Kate recalled that evening when she had told her of her engagement to Simon. So happy, so certain that marriage would soon follow ... After several minutes Joanna raised a pale, wet face.

'I'm sorry, I didn't intend to create a scene.' She made a move to go. 'It was selfish of me to burden you with my problem, I won't take up any more of your time.'

She looked so drawn and tired that Kate felt a wave of compassion for the young girl. 'I've got an idea. Give me five minutes to juggle a couple of appointments and I'll take you home to my flat. You can stay the night with me.'

Joanna protested, but Kate was decisive. 'You look exhausted. What you need is a good night's rest.' She placed an arm about her shoulders. 'Your absence might even make Simon have second thoughts.'

Joanna shook her head miserably. 'There's no chance of that, he's gone for good.'

'All the more reason why you shouldn't be alone in an empty flat tonight.'

'If you're sure . . .' she said uncertainly.

Throughout the journey home Joanna sat silently staring out of the taxi window, meekly submitting to Kate's directions as they alighted and paid their fare. Dismissing the suggestion of a hot bath, she followed Kate through the sitting room to the spare bedroom and lay fully clothed across the bed, silent and dejected. Soon she fell asleep, and as Kate covered the small pale figure with an eiderdown, she thought of the heartache and disillusionment Joanna would wake up to and hoped against hope that she had been mistaken about her brother.

It was inconceivable. Knowing him now as she did, Kate believed Chester to be a rational and considering man. But she could not help feeling a chill of apprehension as she recalled her first meeting with him; his threatening behaviour towards Simon Forrest and her subsequent transfer. Hadn't that been the action of a tough and ruthless man? All in a moment, a charming and courteous man had become angrier than she would have thought possible. She had found it hard to reconcile those two different facets of his character, and instead had pushed all memory of it out of her mind. She had almost succeeded, until today. Now, after hearing Joanna's accusation, at the back of her mind there lingered a suspicion . . .

An hour later Kate was back in her office, a blank piece of paper occupying her attention. For Joanna's sake she must speak to Chester. For her *own* peace of mind she must know the truth, know if the man she loved was capable of behaving in such a ruthless manner. She picked up the telephone, dialled a number, then immediately replaced the receiver. Shock tactics, she decided, were the only way of knowing the truth.

Chester was standing by the window when Kate entered his office, shoulders hunched, hands in his pockets, watching the rain beat against the windows. He motioned her towards a chair and sat opposite. 'Joanna has told you?'

She nodded. 'I thought you ought to know that she's staying with me for a few days.'

'With you?'

'Simon has broken off their engagement and I thought it best she . . .'

'Broken off their engagement?' He was silent, thinking about it, his brow furrowed. 'I suppose the legacy turned out to be smaller than he expected.'

'How can you say that!' Kate exclaimed.

'Don't tell me you haven't *thought* it?'

'What does it matter what either of us think about Simon Forrest . . . Joanna's world has fallen about her ears.'

'She'll get over it,' he shrugged.

'Is that all you can say?' Kate burst out.

'Please believe me, Kate, if there'd been any other way . . .'

'So it's true what Joanna said! You don't deny it?'

He paused a moment, frowned and said: 'What has she told you?'

'That it was you who persuaded Sinclair to dismiss Simon.'

He narrowed his eyes. 'Nothing else?'

'Isn't that enough?'

'*You* appear to think so.'

'What do you expect me to think?' she exclaimed, not heeding the edge to his voice, 'knowing that you used your influence in such a mean way.'

Chester studied a paper-knife on his desk. 'That's what you believe?'

'Well, isn't it true? Isn't it true you arranged to see Sinclair yesterday?'

'He made arrangements to see me. Not entirely the same thing.'

'But all the same in the end, and now two people's lives have been shattered.'

'I wouldn't be so sure about Simon's,' he said indifferently.

'To hell with Simon Forrest! It's Joanna I care about and the heartache she's going through. If what she say's is true . . .'

His fingers tightened about the paper-knife. 'You seem determined to believe her version . . . Simon's version.'

Kate made a despairing movement with her hands.

'But you haven't told me yours.'

He didn't answer at once, but finally he spoke in a tired, defeated voice. 'I shouldn't have to, Kate. If I'm to defend myself to you, then we don't really stand much of a chance, do we?'

He swivelled his chair and watched the streaming panes, his face hidden. His words had sent a stab of anguish through her and in the silence that followed she felt desolation sweep over her. On Joanna's behalf she had thrown down a challenge, forgetting the toughness and determination that lay behind Chester's languid manner and boyish good looks, and now on Joanna's behalf she had lost more than a job. She sat motionless, fighting to control her breathing, tightening her hold on the edge of her chair, knowing that one glance from him and she would retract everything, but his silence and stillness told her she had gone too far and that the situation was beyond apology.

After several moments he turned and looked at her directly, his mouth set in a hard line.

'How long will Joanna be staying with you?' he asked.

'I hope to persuade her to stay a couple of weeks. She's in no state to be left alone.'

'Naturally, I'll settle any expenses you might incur on Joanna's behalf. If you let Miss Johnson have the relevant information, I'll get her to draw up a cheque today.'

'Another file closed and assigned to the OUT tray, is that it? How neat and simple life must appear to you!' Kate said bitterly.

'Not all of us can afford to indulge ourselves . . . Life has to go on and it has to be paid for.'

'Money,' said Kate contemptuously. 'Your answer to everything.'

'Joanna and Simon appeared to think likewise . . . though most times it happened to be *my* money.'

'All that Joanna really wanted was Simon Forrest.'

'Ah, but was Joanna all that Simon wanted?'

'He'd asked her to marry him, isn't that proof enough?' she bristled. 'Not all men treat marriage as a taboo subject.'

'Not all men treat marriage with the respect it's due, if they did the world might be a better place.'

'Well, at least he *asked* her, which must say something in his favour.'

'If you're so sure he loved her, why did he leave?' She opened her mouth as if to speak, but nothing came out. 'Such a pity you haven't experienced a little more of the world, Kate, our relationship might have worked.'

'If it meant having to share my life with an uncaring, unfeeling monster, then I'm thankful to be so unworldly,' she said with extreme bitterness.

His face hardened and he stood up slowly, his voice controlled. 'I think that concludes the matter, don't you? Shall I ring for Miss Johnson or can you see yourself out?'

Kate stood up, her eyes blazing. 'Rest assured I won't bother *you* again!'

'I think that arrangement would suit both of us.'

She turned on her heel to go, but before she had reached the door he said quietly: 'Would you tell Joanna I'd like to see her?'

'As long as you don't make it my place.'

'I'd like to see her.'

'That's her decision,' she said in an indifferent voice, and slammed the door behind her.

CHAPTER ELEVEN

THE tears did not come until later that evening. Later, when her anger had diminished and his words came back with brutal clarity, she wept uncontrollably. That night and many nights to come, until the pain became a dull ache and weariness descended upon her like a black cloud.

At Kate's insistence, Joanna continued to stay on indefinitely in the spare room, but the girl's pale presence was to be a constant reminder of Chester and his callous behaviour towards Simon. Might there have come a time, Kate wondered, when she too would have been treated in such a heartless manner? She thought of her first meeting with Chester and her subsequent transfer. Hadn't that been the action of a tough and ruthless man? The bitter irony of it all was that it should come as a surprise to her.

As the weeks and months passed Kate slowly learned to adjust, resolutely thrusting her thoughts aside and applying herself to her work and, in particular, the French promotion. Pressure of deadlines and meetings allowed her no time to think, but as well as helping her through the day, the hard work started to show results. Fashion writers began to take notice of the new department and to applaud its fresh approach, while sales continued to escalate. At a time of economic recession and battling sales figures, Kate's ability to produce profit was being seen as something of a personal triumph.

A further visit to Paris to hurry along deliveries, plus a generous travel allowance, gave her the opportunity and cash to buy several new outfits, all of which helped to lift her spirits a little, as well as earning male approval about the office. She had decided to take each day as it came, to plan for nothing, for nobody, but with her obvious physical attractions and sympathetic manner, there was no shortage of invitations, and before long her evenings began to be filled.

Only at night, when she had closed her bedroom door on the rest of the world, did desolation sweep over her. During the day work absorbed all her energies, but at night she would lie awake, staring unseeing at the ceiling, isolated in her misery. There were moments when she believed she had come to terms with the reality of their separation, but then she would remember the things Chester had said to her, the loving ecstasy they had shared together, and she ached to feel his body close to hers, to see again the longing in his dark eyes. Only now it was too late.

Although several of her colleagues knew of her friendship with his sister, Kate's brief involvement with Chester had been well concealed, and now as she went about her daily routine she felt able to keep her feelings under control. To others working alongside, she appeared to function as normal, and to the few who might notice her momentary lapses of good temper and the dark rings about her eyes, her excuse was pressure of work.

Social functions were another matter. The light-hearted gathering of a people united in cause and complaint would invariably lead to gossip, and rag trade gossip never failed to touch upon Chester Jones and his latest exploits. Kate always knew that such a man would have little problem finding female consolation, but nevertheless her stomach would tighten into a knot whenever mention was made of his glamorous companions.

Most difficult of all was concealing her emotions from Joanna. Withdrawn and distant, Joanna preferred her own company most evenings, alone in her room, but there were moments when her despair spilled over and she would seek a sympathetic listener, but to sit and listen to Joanna tearfully expounding on the subject of her brother became more than Kate could bear. Fearful of revealing her true feelings on these occasions, she began to spend longer hours at work; travelling to the branches, helping with stock, or simply working overtime in the office.

Late one Friday evening Christopher called her into his office.

'What's new, Kate?'

'One of the Sunday heavies is doing an article on the French actress Marianne Jourdan, and want to feature her in several of our outfits. They're sending her along tomorrow with their photographer.' She smiled. 'I thought you might like to supervise that particular session. Oh, I almost forgot, I'm hoping to tie up something with the French Trade Delegation . . .'

He lay back in his chair, fiddling with a paperclip. 'I wasn't meaning work in particular.'

Kate wrapped her arms around the files she was holding. 'Let me think. There was dinner with Robert Redford on Monday, followed by tea at the Ritz with Michael Caine on Tuesday . . .'

He smiled. 'Apart from that.'

She brushed back her hair. 'Apart from that, I've been too busy.'

'That's what worries me.' He frowned. 'All that work.'

'But I *enjoy* it.'

'That worries me even more. A girl like you should be *out* enjoying yourself, not hunched over figure work late at night.' His grin broadened. 'Having employees who work longer hours than I do makes me nervous.'

'Are you offering me an assistant or your job?' asked Kate lightheartedly.

'A job, if you're interested,' he announced abruptly, offering her a chair and a cigarette.

Bemused, Kate took both and wondered what form of exile Chester had planned for her this time. Christopher pushed a computer sheet towards her.

'Have you seen this week's sales figures for the department?'

'Not in detail, but I understand they're pretty good.'

He nodded. 'So good that everyone believes the French department should be a permanent feature, not simply a seasonal promotion.'

'Would that be viable?'

'Mr Jones appears to think so.' He hesitated. 'In fact, he wants you to take sole responsibility for setting up similar operations in each of our major branches. Buying, as well as publicity, to be in your hands. Of course, it's quite an assignment and you'd have to have an assistant—more than one, if necessary . . .' He paused for her reaction. When it did not come, he continued. 'Of course, you don't have to give me your answer this evening.' His face creased into a grin. 'Just make sure you say yes tomorrow!'

Kate felt too stunned to speak. What possible reason could Chester have for offering her a buyership now? A thought crossed her mind. With Kate neatly out of the way, it would not be difficult to manoeuvre Erika into the publicity department and eventually oust Christopher. Well, if that was how things stood then she and Chester deserved each other and Kate would be only too pleased to leave the field open.

'I thought I would be bringing you good news . . .' observed Christopher wryly.

'It's just that I always seem to be on somebody's transfer list,' Kate sighed.

'Makes you feel unloved and unwanted, does it?'

She smiled wanly. 'Something along those lines.'

'Well, I can assure you that isn't the case. You'll agree

too when you see the terms Tom Preston is offering you.'

She shook her head. 'I'm still not sure.'

'Perhaps Tom can persuade you otherwise on Monday. In the meantime go home and put your feet up. You deserve a break after all that hard work you've put in.'

'I'll take that last piece of advice and think about the first while I'm doing it.'

She stood up and walked towards the door. 'Have a good weekend.'

'You too . . . and Kate . . .' She popped her head back around the door. 'My regards to Robert Redford when you next see him!'

A weekend visit home blew away some of the cobwebs and on Monday morning Kate presented herself in Tom Preston's office, still doubtful, but willing to be persuaded.

'Christopher tells me you have misgivings about the job. Perhaps this will change your mind.' He handed her a new contract showing her revised salary. She raised her eyebrows at the figure. 'You're right,' said Tom, 'it's a lot of money.'

'I can't believe I'm worth this.'

'Chester Jones appears to think so.' He sat back in his chair. 'And I'm inclined to agree with him. A good buyer can make a lot of money for Bennett's and, what's more important, a lot of money for herself.'

Just for a handful of silver, thought Kate.

'You still don't seem convinced. Why not talk it over with Molly Cunningham? You trust her opinion, don't you?'

She nodded. 'We had planned to have lunch together.'

'Perfect.' He jumped up and came around the desk to where she sat. 'Make it somewhere nice. Bennett's will foot the bill . . . and take all the time you need.'

Lunch turned out to be an extravagant affair. Tom Preston's secretary had reserved a table for them both at a nearby hotel, whose elegant and refined surroundings guaranteed them an undisturbed meal. Molly was in a jovial mood and Kate was pleased to be in her company, away from the misery and confusion of her own thoughts.

'I understand this is to be something of a celebration lunch?' smiled Molly, holding up her spectacles to study the large glossy menu.

'Then you might be eating it under false pretences,' said Kate, explaining her reluctance to accept the buyership and her suspicions of Erika's unsubtle hand in the whole proceedings.

Molly sighed and took off her spectacles. 'My dear Kate, where do you get these strange ideas? Chester Jones is director of buying because he's an astute businessman. If he offers you a buyership it's because he knows you have the vision and courage to be a damn good one and not because of the last pretty girl to whisper in his ear. Now . . .' she signalled to one of the waiters, 'let's indulge in a little celebration drink—and don't let me hear any more nonsense about refusing the sort of job any other girl would give her eye teeth for!'

Kate felt a wave of gratitude for the woman sitting opposite her; realising then just how much she had needed Molly's sense of reality, what with her own so blurred and confused.

'You're right, of course. I'll see Tom directly after lunch.'

Seeing Molly had dispelled some of her melancholy, and that evening Kate decided to do the same for Joanna. Nick Garrett, the current darling of the clubs and gossip columns, was about to unveil his latest collection; a theatrical event not to be missed. London was holding its breath and Kate was holding two tickets. For her the show was all part of a long day's work, but she felt sure it would be a social occasion Joanna would enjoy. Through business dealings Kate knew Nick well, she also knew he was planning to move into new showrooms in need of decorations.

When Kate first made the suggestion, Joanna hesitated.

'What if there's anyone I know . . . who might know Simon?'

'All the more reason to show your face,' urged Kate. 'Let it be seen you don't care.'

'But I do.'

'They don't need to know that. Let them think it's Simon's problem and not yours.'

'Maybe you're right,' conceded Joanna, but made one more attempt. 'I don't have anything to wear.'

'No problem. You can choose something of mine.'

When Joanna presented herself at the office the following day, Kate was pleased to see that in spite of her initial reservations, she had made an effort. Her hair had been washed and she had fitted herself into one of Kate's knitted dresses. She looked pretty enough to draw a whistle of appreciation from Christopher, who was passing through.

'Who's the lucky man, then? Or should I say men?'

'Nicky Garret. He's showing his collection this evening at Brook House.'

He glanced at his wristwatch. 'If you can hold on for five minutes I'll drop you off in my car. It's on my way home.' He popped his tousled head back round the door. 'How about joining me for a drink first?'

Christopher's lighthearted mood was catching, and by the time they had reached their destination both girls were in high spirits. The small reception hall was already packed tight with people talking at the tops of their voices; the professionals who were there for the collection, and the 'poseurs' who flitted like moths around every fashionable event, competing among themselves for the next day's headlines. Kate pushed her way through the milling crowd towards a narrow staircase, that enabled them to have a better view of the proceedings.

'To think I used to do this for a living!' whispered Joanna, using her programme as a fan.

Later that evening, after his new collection had received a rapturous reception, Kate succeeded in catching Nicky's attention.

'Darling!' He took hold of her hand and put it to his lips. 'What did you think?'

Kate smiled her congratulations.

'Don't I deserve a department all to myself at Bennett's? I simply can't bear to see my beautiful creations hanging alongside rubbish.'

Kate smiled and gently withdrew her hand. 'Allocating floor space isn't my responsibility, Nick, but having seen what's on offer I'd say you stood a good chance.'

He stood with one hand on his hip and the other stroking his hair. 'I'll be honest with you, Kate. Freeman's are after me for an exclusive franchise. Naturally I'd prefer an arrangement with Bennett's— you do have a touch more class, but they might make me an offer I can't refuse . . .'

Kate dug him playfully in the ribs. 'That's plain hustling, Nick.'

He turned to Joanna in mock horror. 'Did you hear what she called me? A plain hustler! There's nothing plain about Nick Garret. My worst enemy will admit I'm pretty.' Joanna's laugh caught his attention. 'You haven't introduced me to *your* pretty companion, Kate. Is she buying or selling? It affects my conversation.'

'Neither,' smiled Kate, 'Joanna is an interior decorator.'

He threw both hands into the air. 'My dear, do I have a problem you can solve!'

Five minutes later other guests had claimed his attention, but he had left his new address and arrangements for Joanna to meet him there the following day.

'What am I going to do when he finds out?' whispered Joanna.

'Finds out what?'

'That I'm not what you said I am.'

'But you are. You've just never been paid for it.'

The thought depressed her for only a moment.

'Oh, well, I suppose the worst he can do is throw me out.'

'It's important you get a foot in the door, any door. How do you think Nick got started?'

'By being so pretty?' giggled Joanna.

Kate placed a reassuring hand on her arm. 'Don't worry. Nick won't. Simply come up with a scheme on paper and he can say yes or no.' She shrugged. 'Either way you've lost nothing.'

Joanna leant forward and kissed Kate affectionately on the cheek. 'Bless you! I don't know how I could have survived these weeks without you.' Even as she spoke her smile disappeared and she groaned at something she had seen over Kate's shoulder.

'Joanna! How nice to see you back in circulation. Is it business or pleasure?'

Erika Gibbs was wearing a well-cut gentleman's evening suit, but the revealing blouse beneath left no one in any doubt as to her true gender.

'It was pleasurable up to a moment ago,' Joanna mumbled into her drink.

'Joanna's here on business,' interceded Kate. 'Nick Garret is one of her clients.'

'How exciting. What is it you're selling?'

'Wouldn't you like to know?' snapped Joanna.

A faint flush appeared on Erika's cheeks. 'Not really.

I was simply making polite conversation.'

'What would you know of social niceties? People like you don't make polite conversation. You simply feign interest to acquire information.'

Erika addressed herself to Kate. 'It never ceases to amaze me how a gentleman like Chester has such an ill-mannered sister.'

'Too much of a gentleman to tell you to get lost, don't you mean?'

There was a moment's silence.

'He's not like Simon, if that's what you're suggesting, but then you really can't compare our relationship with yours.'

Joanna snorted. 'Relationship! What relationship? You're both in the same business and that's as far as it goes. Will ever go . . .'

'You'd like to think so, wouldn't you?' sneered Erika.

'I know so. I know my own brother.'

Erika smiled across at Kate. 'Heaven preserve us from the certainties of youth!'

'You wouldn't know about that, would you?' said Joanna. 'Your own youth being so long ago.'

'In a civilised society, people like you are usually put on show at fairgrounds,' snapped Erika. If you'll excuse me, I'm meeting Chester for dinner . . .'

Joanna scowled at Erika's retreating back. 'If I'd known she was going to be here I wouldn't have come.'

'And missed the opportunity of your very first client? That's not how empires are built. Besides, we've probably left her wondering.'

'You're right. She's not worth worrying about.' Joanna shook her head. 'I wish I knew what Chester sees in her. What the fascination is.'

'Is he fascinated?' murmured Kate, not really wanting to know the answer.

Joanna shrugged. 'What other explanation is there?'

'You can't deny she's a very attractive woman.'

'I can,' retorted Joanna. 'Have you ever seen her without her make-up?'

'For someone who wasn't going to let it bother her, I'd say that was a particularly bitchy remark,' smiled Kate.

'She is a bitch.'

'Then wouldn't you say that she and Chester deserve each other?'

'Nobody deserves *her*. Not even my brother.'

'That's not the impression you've given me.'

'Oh, I'll admit he deserves the rack and thumbscrews treatment, but not a life sentence.' Then Joanna added in a more serious tone: 'He is my brother and I can't dismiss his good qualities.'

Kate wished she would. Hearing Joanna continually revile Chester and his actions made it easier to build a protective shield around her own emotions. To hear him spoken of with affection would be more than she could bear.

Late into the night the two girls sat around the kitchen table with mugs of hot chocolate, discussing the evening's events. Kate listened as Joanna eagerly expounded on possible ideas for Nick Garret's flat and envied the girl's enthusiasm. Would the time ever come again when she too would feel that way about something? Someone?

But the new job began to demand more of her time and attention, and a pretence at preoccupation gradually gave way to total absorption in her work. The success of the French campaign continued unabated and Kate found herself swept up in a whirlwind of activity; the department increased its footage in London and spread to all major branches, the promised assistant became several and Kate's trips to Paris became a regular shuttle.

The new venture continued to attract the attention of

the Press, who knew that professional success wrapped in a young and glamorous package always made good reading. On several occasions her fresh ideas and sympathetic manner proved successful on local radio, and to her surprise she started to enjoy every frantic moment of it.

She had not seen Chester since their separation, and now, as the weeks went by, work and exhaustion left little time for reflection. Even tearful reminders from Joanna grew fewer, engrossed as she was in her first assignment as an interior designer. By degrees, life was beginning to feel worthwhile: one morning Kate had woken up and thought first of the day ahead and not of the time past, and she knew she had returned to the land of the living.

Christmas came and went and Kate received in the office post a party invitation for New Year's Eve. Each year, at this time, Molly held open house for all her friends and the occasion had become something of a traditional event, but knowing for certain that Chester would have been invited, Kate felt her heart fill with fear at the prospect. To ask outright would possibly arouse Molly's suspicions and not to accept her invitation would be unthinkable. Besides, Molly had given everyone several weeks' notice. Kate sighed. It was impossible to go on dreading a meeting with Chester and perhaps, as his employee, it was best to face him first on neutral territory.

'Why not ask Alain?' Molly had suggested. 'It can't be much fun celebrating the New Year on your own in a foreign country.'

Alain Boivin had become one of the few bright spots on Kate's cloudy horizon. His increased involvement with the French Department had been inevitable, his courteous manner a welcome contrast to the usual fractious proceedings, so that Kate looked forward to seeing him on his frequent visits to London. Over the weeks and months a close working relationship grew up be-tween them both and once he had tentatively spoken of deeper feelings for her, but she had smiled away his advances and blamed the excellence of the burgundy they were enjoying at the time.

'I wish I could persuade you to work in France,' he told her.

'Absence makes the heart grow fonder.'

He threw up his hands in a despairing gesture. 'So English!'

'I can't help it,' she laughed. 'I am English.'

'And I can't help feeling about you the way I do.'

'My mother warned me against foreigners, especially the passionate sort.' Kate wrinkled her nose. 'I suspect she once succumbed to an Italian on a trip to Florence with her parents . . . They, my grandparents that is, had intended the trip to be a cultural one . . . She probably learned a lot more than they intended.'

'I wish her daughter would succumb,' sighed Alain.

'A few girls in the office would. You should hear what some of them think about you!'

'Why don't you ever take me seriously, Kate?'

Why? Because laughter and jokes were a way of keeping the real world at arm's length; being serious meant having to face harsh realities. Perhaps Alain had spoken the truth when he told her of his feelings, but she wasn't about to take that chance . . . ever again. At least, not yet awhile. Seeing his glum look she reached for his hand. 'Molly has asked me to her New Year's party. Why not come along?'

'Would Molly mind?'

'She wants you to come. Asked for you especially.'

'Do *you* want me to?'

Kate smiled warmly and squeezed his hand. 'I wouldn't go without you.'

In the weeks following his sudden departure there had

been no news of Simon Forrest. No attempt by him to explain or apologise for his precipitous action. In his absence, and with Joanna's increasing absorption in her new interest, the stormy relationship between Chester Jones and his sister had lost something of its impetus and had gradually subsided. Both had spent Christmas with relatives in Switzerland, but Joanna had decided to delay her homecoming until after the New Year. In her telegram to Kate she made no mention of her brother's plans, and Kate wondered if Chester would be staying also. If so, there was no likelihood of his attending Molly's party.

For the man who might not be there she chose her dress with great care; a simple black sheath she had bought in Paris and deliberately kept aside for such an occasion. The soft silk skimmed lightly over her figure, barely suggestive of the curves beneath, at variance with the low-cut bodice that revealed the swell of her full breasts. The effect was stunning in its simplicity. Any doubts she might have had as to the neckline being too low were swept aside by Alain's look of approval as she opened the door to him.

'Do we have to go to the party?' he teased, his eyes appreciative of her curvaceous outline.

'You don't think it's too revealing?' she asked hesitantly. 'I could wear this.'

He waved aside the fine lace shawl. 'A beautiful woman should never hide the fact . . .' He drew her arm through his. 'This evening all Englishmen will wish me back in France!'

Alain's enthusiasm had been infectious, but as soon as Molly ushered them into the midst of the festivities, Kate knew she had made a mistake. All day she had felt uneasy and now, swamped by inconsequential chatter and nodding acquaintances, she wished desperately she had not agreed to come, but for Molly's sake she determined to raise some semblance of enjoyment. One large champagne cocktail helped to steady her nerves and resolution, and after two she began to feel relaxed.

'Molly has a wide circle of friends,' said Alain, nodding towards the numerous guests, some of whom had begun to spill out from the main room into the hall.

'I believe they started off as small intimate dinner parties and like Topsy, just growed,' laughed Kate.

The atmosphere of the room had grown warm and oppressive, and Kate decided to deposit the shawl she had surreptitiously placed about her shoulders in the car. She excused herself to Alain, who was deep in conversation with a business acquaintance, and slipped away to Molly's bedroom. When she made her way back he was still immersed in his discussion, but not until she had drawn closer did she recognise the tall, familiar figure now at his side. She caught her breath, but even as she hesitated Chester Jones turned and caught her scrutiny.

'Kate! Good evening. I was just congratulating Alain on the results you've both achieved this season.'

His tone was formal and correct, but simply hearing him speak her name had been sufficient to remind her and she felt unable to speak. There was an awkward pause as she felt his eyes upon her, then Alain laid a solicitous arm about her waist.

'I've been telling Chester how well we work together.'

'It seems to be an arrangement that works well for Bennett's,' observed Chester.

'And for me too,' smiled Alain.

'You made a wise decision, Kate, coming back to buying.'

'I never wanted to leave in the first place, if you remember?'

'I remember, and I'm man enough to admit I made a mistake transferring you.'

'All of us make mistakes in the heat of the moment . . .' she shrugged.

'So I'm forgiven?'

She looked straight at him. 'As far as I'm concerned that's all in the past, and lots of things in the past are best forgotten.'

She had spoken as casually as she could, but the underlying truth was understood by them both.

'No regrets, then?'

'No regrets.'

Kate drew a sigh of relief as Tom Preston and another man joined their circle, seeking Chester's opinion on a recent merger, and as soon as politely possible she discreetly withdrew. Coming face to face with Chester like that had left her unnerved and flustered, and she momentarily sought her own company in a quiet corner of the room. Without even trying he had stirred into life feelings she thought she had reasoned away, but she had been a fool to suppose otherwise.

Scarcely had her body stopped trembling when she became conscious of a figure at her elbow. Hardly daring to do so, Kate turned and looked up at the man standing beside her.

'I haven't had a chance to thank you for helping Joanna,' said Chester, speaking in an undertone that excluded others. 'She appears to be making quite a success of her new job.'

'I only made the first introduction, her own talent did the rest,' said Kate.

'In my eyes that's no mean achievement ... seeing Joanna actually enjoy work.'

'Oh, she enjoys working all right. It's the emptiness in between she can't handle.'

He swirled his drink slowly. 'What I did was for the best, Kate.'

'Whose best? Joanna's? Your own?'

He made no answer and in the silence that followed she looked away, hoping he had not noticed the tremor of her lower lip. The coming and going of guests had pushed them together and now, standing very close, Kate felt his eyes lingering upon the swelling lines of her breasts and her whole body filled with longing.

'I'd almost forgotten how beautiful you were . . .'

He spoke in little more than a whisper, and Kate trembled slightly at the strange expression in his eyes as they rested on her bare throat and the gold chain that hung about it.

'You still wear my charm,' he commented.

'Yours?'

'You lost it, remember?'

'I was careless . . . It won't happen again.'

He studied his drink. 'You're still angry with me. Perhaps if you knew the truth you'd understand why I acted the way I did.'

'What sort of truth is it that causes such unhappiness?'

'An ugly truth, Kate. One I hope Joanna doesn't have to learn.'

As they spoke the svelte figure of Erika Gibbs had appeared in Kate's line of vision and was moving slowly but resolutely in their direction.

'Kate,' she drawled, leading Alain by the arm, 'you really should take more care of this Frenchman. He's much too dangerous to be let loose in mixed company!'

'I thought that was all part of a Frenchman's appeal,' observed Chester lightheartedly. 'Why else do you suppose the women of England voted overwhelmingly to join the Common Market?'

Erika laughed and affectionately slipped her arm through Chester's. 'Chester tells me you're having to spend a great deal of your time in France these days, Kate.'

'Not enough time, as far as I'm concerned,' smiled Alain, moving closer to Kate.

'Didn't I tell you he was dangerous, Chester? Having handsome Frenchmen entice away your buyers must be the quickest way you know of reducing staff over-heads.'

'A simple transfer works even faster,' murmured Kate.

For the rest of the evening Kate moved numbly about the room, detached from the laughter and revelry that washed around her, ever conscious of Chester's presence somewhere about her. Once she had looked up and found him watching her, but she turned away contemptuously, steadfastly refusing to look in his direction. Her confrontation with him had sapped her energies and she made her way to the bar, in need of a drink to steady her nerves. Molly was playing host; balancing a cigarette in one hand and a tray of drinks in the other. 'Help yourself, Kate. It's almost twelve and I have to make certain everyone has a glass of champagne.'

Towards midnight the noise grew steadily louder and the room hotter, and Kate decided to slip away into the small garden. As she stood in the shadows a figure appeared in the doorway, hesitated a moment, then walked towards her.

'You seem to be missing all the fun out here,' said Chester, motioning towards the flat filled with noisy revellers.

A look of disdain crossed her face. 'That *was* my intention.'

'Just as I thought, so . . .' he held up a bottle of champagne, 'I've bought some of the fun outside. If you would just hold these . . .' He held out two glasses.

'Hadn't it occurred to you I might prefer my own company?' she said coldly.

'Don't argue, Kate. It's almost twelve.'

'Yours least of all . . .'

He smiled softly as he poured the champagne, ignoring her protests.

'Arguing with your boss is no way to win promotion,

and certainly no way to celebrate the New Year. Now . . .' His face had grown suddenly serious and she held her breath as she felt him draw close, 'Happy New Year, Kate.'

'Happy New Year, Chester.'

In the silence that followed he took her glass and placed it beside him, then laid his hands on her bare shoulders. 'I prefer my own way of seeing in the New Year.' He drew her to him and his lips came down on hers, soft and lingering. At length they stood apart, but his hands remained, lightly caressing her shoulders. 'It's been a long time, Kate . . .'

She thought she had learned to live without him; had managed to convince herself that their time together had just been part of some shadowy dream, but seeing Chester again had proved otherwise and at that moment, more than anything else, she wanted things to be as they were, wanted to feel his arms locked tightly about her and to drown beneath his kisses, but it was too late, and instead she twisted away from him.

'I have to find Alain. He'll be wondering where I am.'

'He seems to be very fond of you?'

'Yes.'

'And you?' he queried.

'As you said, it's been a long time . . .'

'Is he serious?'

There was a moment's pause as her eyes met his.

'He wants me to live with him in France . . .'

'He wants you to *marry* him?'

'Got it in one.'

She had spoken with an intentional cruelty, but now, when she saw the stunned look on his face, she immediately regretted her impulsive remark. But in a moment his eyes had hardened.

'Erika wants to spend our honeymoon in France . . . somewhere hot and south.'

She held on to her glass tightly, willing her hands to remain steady.

'You and she plan to marry?'

'As soon as we find a house.'

'What's wrong with your flat?' asked Kate, straining to keep her voice steady.

'Erika wants a house with a garden. Something more suitable for a family.'

'Does Joanna know of your plans?' asked Kate.

'No . . .' He hesitated, combing back his hair with his fingers. 'I was rather hoping you would break the news to her.'

'Me?'

'She has such a high regard for you, Kate. I know she'd listen to you.'

'No . . . no . . .' protested Kate, vehemently shaking her head. Tell me it isn't true, her heart pleaded. Tell me it isn't true.

Chester shrugged a shoulder. 'I'm sorry, I shouldn't have asked you, but knowing how close you and Joanna have become . . .'

He went on to explain himself, but she heard nothing. She had already heard enough; the man she loved most in all the world was planning to marry someone else, and that someone else was Erika Gibbs! As Chester was speaking Alain's anxious figure appeared in the doorway, and suddenly all that Kate wanted was to put distance between herself and the man standing before her, and she didn't look back as she hurried across the lawn and into Alain's arms.

'Darling!' she called, forcing a note of pleasure into her voice. 'You haven't wished me a Happy New Year.'

'I've been looking everywhere for you.'

'You can't have been looking very hard, the flat's tiny and the garden even smaller.'

Alain glanced across at the solitary figure at the far end of the garden. 'I wasn't sure you wanted to be found.'

Kate made no answer, but as their eyes met his face melted into comprehension, and she was grateful he left unsaid what was understood by them both. 'You're shivering. Would you like me to get your wrap?'

CHAPTER TWELVE

THE morning after the party Alain had returned to Paris, and Kate felt strangely vulnerable without him, withouts his warmth and understanding. One Sunday morning, two weeks later, the telephone bell jangled its way into her sleep and announced his return.

'Are you free for lunch?' he asked her.

'I've a driving lesson at twelve. Could we meet later?'

'Let's make it afternoon tea. Somewhere on the river, perhaps?'

'That will be lovely,' mumbled Kate sleepily, glad that he had called and that they were to remain friends.

They decided upon a small whitewashed hotel, tucked away in a tranquil river setting, where green lawns sloped gently down to the water's edge. The perfect setting to while away a warm summer's day, but in January, with the chilling presence of an easterly wind and a cosy fire burning in the old-fashioned panelled dining room, few lingered outside to admire the view. Tea was served on crisp white cloths; China tea, with scones and various jams, along with the Sunday papers. Their mood was a relaxed and happy one, but towards the end of their meal, a thoughtful expression appeared on Alain's face.

'I don't believe you've heard one word I've said this afternoon. What's wrong, Kate?'

She forced a smile, taken aback by the unexpected turn of their conversation.

'Wrong?' she queried.

'You are troubled about something . . . about somebody? For a long time now.'

He paused. 'Would it help to talk about it?'

She didn't answer at once, unwilling to reveal her secret, but the kindness and concern in his voice weakened her resolve.

'It's a long story.'

'Confession is good for the soul,' smiled Alain.

With a feeling almost of relief, Kate took a deep breath and began at the beginning: the fun and excitement of her new career, her first meeting with a tearful Joanna, the brash appearance of Simon Forrest and his part in the whole proceedings, her own subsequent involvement with the Jones family ... and then she told him about Chester. Alain listened in silence to her story, his face revealing nothing of his thoughts. When she had finished he sat for a moment considering her words.

'I wish you had told me sooner ... trusted me more. It would have helped you to talk things over.'

'I can see that now, but at the time everything seemed so unreal, part of some shadowy dream. Even now you might think it sounds like the workings of an over-fertile imagination.'

'It *sounds* like a French farce; not at all how I expected English people to behave.'

Kate smiled. 'We don't spend all our time drinking tea and playing cricket!'

'Perhaps not, but spending time doing either does suggest a degree of civilised behaviour.'

'Chester Jones does both, which challenges that particular theory.'

Alain shook his head in bewilderment. 'You say it was he who brought about Simon's dismissal? Knowing the man I find that difficult to believe.'

'I don't. Look at the callous way he treated me—simply because I questioned the wisdom of his logic.'

Alain laughed out loud. 'My dear Kate, question a man's virility, his pedigree even, but *never* his logic.' He pushed away his empty tea cup. 'You say his sister is staying with you now?'

'Not for much longer. Chester has offered her his flat.'

'He's moving?'

'I told you, he's planning to get married and he's looking for a house ... somewhere in the country, Joanna tells me.'

Alain frowned. 'That also I cannot understand ...'

'His buying a house in the country?'

'His plans to marry Erika Gibbs.'

'So does Joanna, she's still to be won over. Being offered the flat was only part consolation, but she's young and will eventually come round to accepting Erika as Chester's wife.'

'But will you?' he asked quietly.

'I already have,' she assured him, but he was not fooled by her lighthearted tone.

He beckoned to their waiter to bring the bill.

'Have you any plans for this evening, or would you like to go to the cinema?' he asked.

'I plan to take you home, introduce you to Joanna— if you behave, that is, and to open that beautiful bottle of cognac you brought me from France.'

'And then?'

'Then I shall push you firmly out the door,' smiled Kate. 'I've volumes of paperwork to see to before Monday.'

For the first time in many weeks, purged of her guilty secret, she felt content, and on the journey home she suddenly leant across the car and kissed Alain affectionately on the cheek. He glanced sideways. 'That was nice.'

'So are you.' She slipped her arm through his and laid her head on his shoulder. 'Such a dear, dear friend.'

'I wish I could be more.'

Kate shook her head. 'Friends are more precious than lovers. Love causes misery and unhappiness. Friendship is warm and comforting, like hot chocolate and warm slippers.'

'A girl with your looks and figure deserves more than that!'

She pulled a face and giggled, too happy to feel offended by his compliment.

Joanna was curled up in an armchair when they arrived, absorbed in a book, but at Alain's appearance she sat up straight and tried to bring some order to her dishevelled hair, returning his smile of greeting in full measure. Dressed casually in jeans and a T-shirt, her tousled curls falling about her face, she gave the appearance, almost, of a schoolgirl, but there was something in her smile, in the flicker of those dark upturned eyes, that Kate hadn't seen before that evening. If she didn't know better, she would have supposed the handsome Frenchman was partly to blame.

'He's a charmer,' said Joanna later that evening, when Alain had taken his leave of them both.

'He's a Frenchman,' smiled Kate, seated at her dressing table.

'I read somewhere that it's the garlic that does it,' said Joanna philosophically.

'Or something in their wine,' suggested Kate.

'Mmm . . . seems almost a pity Napolean never got this far.'

'I'm not so sure . . . once married, Frenchmen can be very demanding of their wives; lots of beautifully cooked meals, lots of attention, lots of children . . .'

'My idea of heaven!'

'Not for me,' Kate said firmly, 'I value my freedom too much.'

'What you really mean is that you don't value Alain enough to forfeit your so-called freedom.'

'Possibly . . .'

Joanna lay across the bed, watching Kate brush her hair. 'You're the only woman I know who looks more glamorous when she's taken off her make-up,' she told her.

Kate laughed. 'I've a sneaking suspicion that was meant to be a compliment!'

'There you are, you get so many you don't even notice. I wish I had what you have.'

'Sounds ominous.'

'A flock of admirers was what I meant.'

'Sorry to disappoint you,' said Kate, 'but my score card isn't that impressive.'

Joanna fell on to her back and smiled up at the ceiling. 'Anyone who can afford to be that casual with good-looking Frenchmen automatically impresses me!'

Kate shrugged. 'Mixing emotions with business is never wise.'

'Is that why you and Chester avoid each other?' murmured Joanna, still staring up at the ceiling.

The brush stopped in mid-air. 'Chester and I? I don't know what you're talking about.' Kate resumed brushing her hair, her cheeks burning. 'Sparks might fly between us both, but not the sort you're suggesting.'

Joanna yawned and stretched her arms. 'Oh, I'm not suggesting *you* are attracted to him! I wouldn't be so beastly. No, it's more the way *he* behaves towards you . . . something I can't quite put my finger on . . .'

Kate stood up and playfully pushed her towards the door. 'You're speaking rubbish, Joanna. I suggest your brain is in need of some deep sleep.'

After Joanna had left the room, Kate stood for a moment deep in thought, then appeared to reach a decision.

Alain was invited for lunch the following Sunday at one o'clock. By half past twelve Joanna and Kate had completed all their preparations and were sitting with a glass of sherry. Throughout the morning Joanna had helped with undiminished good nature; plumping cushions, peeling potatoes, polishing glasses. Simple domestic tasks that usually evoked frowns, were hummed and smiled over, and now as she sat opposite, her usual jeans and sneakers discarded for a soft pink dress and slim high heels, Kate thought how pretty she looked with her shining chestnut hair framing those dark family eyes. Youthful exuberance combined with such physical attractions might well prove irresistible, thought Kate.

At ten minutes to one the doorbell rang and Kate was confronted by the smiling face of Alain, who greeted her with a small kiss. 'You smell delicious, or is it the food?' His smile widened to include Joanna.

'It's the food,' laughed Kate. 'Braised lamb and spinach.'

'We hope it's the food,' corrected Joanna. 'But don't worry. If anything goes madly wrong there's a splendid Chinese takeaway at the end of the road.'

'Neither of us are very experienced cooks, I'm afraid,' added Kate.

'With your looks, neither of you has to be.'

'If you're going to say things like that, we must invite you to lunch more often.'

He shrugged his shoulders. 'If the food is as tempting as the cooks, I shall certainly come.'

'Don't say another word until you've eaten,' warned Joanna, 'and then anything you say may be taken down and used in evidence!'

Despite the cooks' initial reservations, lunch proved to be a culinary success; the food and wine agreeing with all three, and as the meal progressed Alain and Joanna chatted away like old friends. The world and its problems finally put to rights over cheese and biscuits, Kate cleared away the empty dishes and served coffee. They had been speaking earlier of Joanna's ventures into decorating, and now Alain pursued the subject further.

'I've recently bought a new flat in Paris—small, but it has interesting possibilities. Myself, I wouldn't know where to begin, and I was wondering if you could suggest anything?'

Joanna pursed her lips. 'I'd hate to commit myself, not having seen the layout of the rooms, which of them are facing north or south ... details like that can make all the difference ...' A smile replaced the frown. 'But of course I'll try.'

'No need to try. Come over and see for yourself.'

Joanna stared in disbelief. 'Come to Paris? Just like that?'

'For a fee, naturally, plus your expenses. I don't expect you to work for nothing.'

She leaned forward and her eyes lit up. 'A job in Paris! I should be paying you.'

Alain smiled at her enthusiasm. 'I take it your answer is yes?'

'My bags are packed!'

Joanna filled their glasses with the remains of the wine and insisted on toasting 'this special occasion', and as Kate sipped her drink and saw the smiles that passed between her two companions, she wondered just how much of a special occasion it might turn out to be.

'I suppose I should speak to your brother,' Alain said thoughtfully.

'Chester? What on earth for?'

'He is my boss and you're his sister.'

She waved aside his protests. 'What you do in your free time is your own business, whatever Chester would have you believe—and as for me, I'm over age and responsible for my actions.'

Kate silently agreed with her, having witnessed that evening a young girl's transformation.

The night before her departure for Paris, bags packed, ticket and passport checked and double-checked and laid out conspicuously on the hall table, Joanna sat on the kitchen table resting her legs on a chair, while Kate cleared away.

'Do you mind my going to Paris?' asked Joanna.

'Mind? Why should I mind?'

'I thought, maybe . . .' Joanna twisted the damp tea towel about her fingers.

'You and Alain being so close, I'd hate you to think . . .'

Kate smiled and placed a reassuring hand over hers. 'I've already told you, Alain is a dear friend, a very dear friend, nothing more.'

'If you're sure?'

'I'm sure. Sure that if you didn't go to Paris you'd regret it for the rest of your life.'

Joanna considered this as she pushed back a stray curl behind her ear. 'Perhaps you're right.' There was a moment's silence as she leant forward and studied her toes. 'Why don't you marry Alain, Kate?'

Kate finished the washing up. 'I don't happen to love him. It's as simple as that.' She untied her apron and laid it across the back of a chair. 'There are some people I'm happy to spend some time with . . . a lot of time, maybe, but the rest of my life?' She shook her head decisively. 'That's something else.'

'Have you ever found that something else? That someone you wanted to spend the rest of your life with?'

Kate nodded. 'But he didn't feel the same way.'

'I can't imagine anyone walking away from you,' said Joanna. 'Now me, that's different.'

'Do you still miss Simon?' asked Kate.

'Of course I do.' Joanna hesitated. 'At least, I think I do. He's been away so long I sometimes think it's the image of unrequited love I'm in love with.'

'You've heard nothing at all from him?'

'Not even a postcard saying "Wish you were here".' Joanna jumped off the table. 'One thing's for sure, he's not missing me!'

Several days after Joanna's departure, Kate was to be called out of a meeting to attend to an urgent phone call. It was Simon, anxious to locate Joanna. Irritated at the interruption and by the man at the other end of the line, Kate was noncommittal, but he was insistent and, unable to discuss the matter over the phone, she arranged to meet him that evening after work. He had suggested a small bar in Covent Garden, at a distance from the office, to avoid any possibility of meeting former acquaintances.

'How are you, Simon?' she asked as she walked up to him.

He spread his hands and attempted a smile. 'I'm all right.'

But he didn't look all right. Gone were the smooth executive jacket and matching slacks, the crisply co-ordinated shirt and tie, and that air of total confidence that had held the whole package together. Something had gone badly amiss for the miserable figure that now sat before her in a wet crumpled raincoat, and Kate hoped, for all their sakes, they had not been wrong about him.

While Simon ordered their drinks Kate went to freshen up, and as she sat combing her hair in the cloakroom Erika Gibbs' reflection appeared suddenly over her shoulder.

'Hello! What are you doing so far from home? I thought only Chester and I knew of this bolt-hole.'

Kate forced a smile, but felt her throat go dry at the realisation that Chester must be close at hand.

'We're grabbing a drink before going on to the theatre.' Erika leant forward to study her features. 'How's Joanna? Gaining quite a reputation for herself, I gather? I met Nick Garret for lunch the other day and he's as pleased as punch with his new showroom.' There was a pause as she concentrated on applying fresh lipstick. 'Of course, I only hear of these things secondhand—she refuses to speak to *me* since Chester told her of our marriage plans, and some of the things she said to Chester don't bear repeating. I admire you for putting up with her this long.' She swivelled the lipstick back into its gilt case. 'Don't worry, she'll be moving into Chester's flat just as soon as we've decided upon the house we want.'

'Joanna tells me he's buying a house in the country,' said Kate.

'He *thinks* he's buying a house in the country, but I refuse to be shut away in some decaying dower house. London suits me fine.'

'Chester told me of your plans . . . I hope you'll both be very happy.'

With something approaching condescension, Erika placed a hand on Kate's shoulder. 'I did try to warn you.'

Kate felt her cheeks flood with colour. 'Warn me?'

'That Chester's interest in you was simply that of a kindly employer for his employee, an employee who was making a lot of money for his company. Nothing more, nothing less.' She gave a small smile. 'If it's any consolation you weren't the first to make the mistake of supposing that concern was something deeper.' She made a final inspection of her face. 'I must go, or Chester will wonder where I've got to.'

Kate stared blankly at her image in the mirror, then closed her eyes to stem the tears, to shut out the image of Chester with that woman, with any woman other than herself. How would she get through the evening?

After what seemed an age, she roused herself and joined Simon. Hardly daring to do so, she looked about her. Then she saw him; a strangely dejected figure, seated with Erika and another couple. He sat smoking with a steady unconcern for his surroundings, oblivious to the hum of conversation about him. He looked up suddenly and met her eyes and even at that distance she saw the flinch. He did not smile, but acknowledged her presence with a curt nod. She turned away and smiled up at Simon as he appeared with their drinks.

'Sorry I've been so long, they had to get some more ice.'

Simon had deliberately chosen a table tucked away in a quiet corner, and as they settled themselves with their drinks, he set about explaining his long absence. He spoke of the pressures he had been under: of Chester's continued opposition, his untimely dismissal from the *Dispatch* and consequent loss of face before Joanna. And now, of his loneliness and regret.

Kate listened politely, but her mind and heart were elsewhere, her body electrically aware of another's presence. To think she had almost forgotten how handsome Chester was; those dark brooding features, at once so forceful yet so sensitive. She tried to shut out the image of Erika sitting beside him. Was he as soft and persuasive to her as he had once been towards Kate? A lifetime seemed to have passed since he had held her in his arms and she had drowned beneath his kisses. And now? Now he had chosen Erika. It didn't make sense, but nothing Kate could say or do would alter that fact.

Later, when she chanced a second look, she was relieved to see Chester and his guests moving towards the entrance doors. She was also relieved that Simon had reached the end of his lengthy explanation.

'So you see I must speak to Joanna,' he was saying.

'Joanna's in Paris at the moment, working.'

'Working?' Simon queried. Kate explained Joanna's new professional status. 'I see . . .' He studied the bottom of his glass. 'She seems to have done pretty well for herself.'

'You've been away a long time, Simon,' she pointed out.

'Do you think she'll see me?'

'I'm afraid I can't answer for Joanna.'

'No, of course not . . .' He shrugged and looked unhappy.

Kate gave a sympathetic smile. 'Leave it with me and I'll see what I can do. She's due back soon and I'll have a word with her.'

It was nine o'clock when Kate arrived home. She felt empty and very tired. Light filtered through the sitting room window and she supposed Joanna to have arrived home earlier than she intended. She wondered what her reaction would be when she learnt of Simon's return. She hurried into her apartment, pleased to have company, but stopped dead as soon as she opened the sitting room door. Chester was leaning against the edge of a table, his arms folded, apparently awaiting her return.

'What on earth . . .' she gasped, thinking she was imagining things.

'I told your landlady I was Joanna's brother and she let me in.'

'How dare you take such liberties! You know full well Joanna's away.'

Recovering a little of her composure, she closed the door after her. 'Aren't you supposed to be at the theatre? Or is frightening me more entertaining?'

'I've told you before, I leave the high living to Erika and her friends.'

Kate slipped her handbag off her shoulder and on to a chair; she was nervous at being alone with him and she hoped it didn't show. 'You and your future wife don't appear to have a great deal in common. Sounds like a very civilised arrangement.'

He looked at her without expression; a man in absolute control. 'At least she doesn't compromise herself with other men in shady nightclubs. But then I suppose Frenchmen are more broadminded.'

Kate felt herself stiffen in sudden defence. 'Alain trusts me.'

'Ah, yes ... trust. Although considering you're an engaged woman, I'm a little surprised at the company you're keeping nowadays.'

She chose an armchair as far as possible from where he stood.

'Who I see in my own time is my own business,' she said with false lightness.

'What does he want?' Chester asked coldly.

'Simon? I'd say that was his business, wouldn't you?'

He suddenly exploded. 'If it concerns Joanna it is *my* business!'

'I wouldn't be too sure of that. Joanna's grown up a lot in these past months. She's become an independent woman with a mind of her own and won't welcome your interference.'

'Aren't you interferring?' he snapped, his voice strained and furious.

'I want what Joanna wants; you want what you want.'

'Before you came along Joanna wasn't sure what she wanted. Now I suspect there's more than a little of your influence in whatever she decides.'

Kate bridled. 'That's unfair! I offered her a home when she had none, and she's been very happy here—perhaps for the first time in her life.'

'Now who's being unfair? As a child she had every-thing she ever wanted.'

'As a child, yes. The only trouble was you wouldn't let her grow up.'

'If growing up meant leading the free and easy life *you* appear to enjoy...'

Kate let a moment pass before she answered, hurt by his spiteful words.

'I don't deserve that,' she whispered.

In the silence that followed his dark eyes held hers and a muscle twitched in the strong jaw. She looked away, afraid of what she might reveal.

'Does Joanna know he's in London?' he asked at last.
'No.'

'Do you have to tell her?'

'She'd find out sooner or later.'

There was a tremor of curiosity in his eyes. 'If it's Joanna he's interested in . . .'

'What's that supposed to mean?'

'If it's Joanna he's interested in, why is he wining and dining you?'

Kate looked dumbstruck; outraged by his insinuation. 'He phoned me at the office today wanting to know of Joanna's whereabouts,' she explained, wondering why she should be justifying herself. 'He was insistent, and the only way to get him off the line and back to my meeting was to see him this evening and hear him out.'

'In some intimate little nightclub where you wouldn't be seen.'

She shook her head in frustration. 'It wasn't like that . . . Simon didn't want to bump into any of his former colleagues.'

'I'm not surprised, the way he's behaved!'

She stood up abruptly. 'Your own behaviour is nothing to be proud of,' she said, with sudden extreme bitterness. 'Not only did you succeed in breaking Joanna's heart, you destroyed Simon's livelihood into the bargain.'

'And you're helping him pick up the pieces, are you? How very romantic!'

'That's a ridiculous thing to say. His only concern is for Joanna, who happens to be out of the country at the moment.'

His voice matched hers. 'How very convenient for you both!'

Kate's eyes blazed. This time he had gone too far, but she did not have the emotional strength to argue. Unable to speak, she flung open the door for him to leave.

He took a step towards her. 'Kate . . .' then he

stopped when he saw the expression on her face. His last words were lost to her as she slammed the door behind him.

CHAPTER THIRTEEN

DESPITE the threat of rain that hung in the air, the drive to the airport was an exhilarating one, as well as giving Kate the perfect excuse to drive her new black sports car. Joanna was returning from Paris that morning and, on the pretext of showing off the car, Kate had arranged to meet her at Heathrow, but in truth she was more than a little anxious to learn how well she and Alain had got on. There was no doubt they had been attracted to each other; how strong that attraction was Kate had yet to find out. If events should turn out as she hoped, Alain might well be the happy solution to several people's problems.

She stood and scanned the faces of new arrivals passing through the Customs, and then she saw her, bright-eyed and smiling, and with a cry of delight Joanna ran forward and kissed her friend affectionately on the cheek.

'I take it your trip was a success,' smiled Kate.

'Wildly! I've overspent, overindulged and feel on top of the world.'

'Paris tends to have that effect on people. That first sip can go straight to your head, if you're not careful.'

'If you're lucky, don't you mean?'

'If you're lucky,' laughed Kate, as she helped to load two suitcases and several large parcels into the car. 'You seem to have brought most of Paris home with you. What's in all these parcels?'

'Lots and lots of clothes.'

'What kind?'

'The expensive kind. Is there any other kind in Paris?

Alain helped me to choose, and just wait 'til you see what we chose for you!'

'Naughty or nice?' asked Kate.

'Depends entirely on the company you keep.'

'Curiouser and curiouser, cried Alice . . . How was the flat, by the way?'

'Flat?'

'The *flat*. The reason you went, remember?'

'Oh, that. I've taken all the measurements, but nothing definite has been resolved. Alain insisted on showing me Paris and I hardly had time to catch my breath: art exhibitions in the morning, markets in the afternoon, then somewhere typically French for dinner.'

'Doesn't sound much like hard work to me,' laughed Kate.

'Nor me,' grinned Joanna, 'but don't tell that to Alain!'

'I thought he might be with you,' said Kate, as she pulled out into the flow of traffic heading towards London.

'He's promised to come next weekend . . .' Joanna hesitated a fraction. 'By then I hope to have a few ideas to show him.'

Rain had begun to fall heavily and faced with the inevitable traffic congestion Kate suggested they pull in at a small pub for lunch. Not until they had eaten several slices of cold beef with a crisp green salad, and their waiter had cleared away, did Kate mention her visitor.

'You got my letter?'

Joanna very carefully set down her glass of wine. 'About Simon?'

'You don't appear surprised.'

'That he's shown up? It was only a matter of time. In his haste to be off he left his passport behind. We'd been planning to go on holiday.'

'He made no mention of a passport,' said Kate. 'Simply wanted to see you.'

'I don't think I want to see him.'

'He was very persistent. He called several times.'

For a long moment Joanna said nothing, then she shook her head. 'It's almost as if I'm afraid of finding out the truth.'

'That you still love him?'

'That I don't. To have gone through all that unhappiness only to discover that.'

'You have to know,' urged Kate. 'You'll never really be free unless you do.'

Joanna nodded. 'For my own sake, for everybody's sake, I must see Simon . . . sooner or later.'

The phone call came early on Sunday morning, and when she heard Joanna's drowsy reply turn suddenly guarded and matter-of-fact Kate knew at once who it was. After several minutes there was the click of the receiver and Joanna's dishevelled figure appeared in the doorway.

'That was Simon. He's calling round this afternoon.'

'He hasn't wasted much time,' commented Kate, propping herself up on one elbow.

'Only two years of my life.'

'This afternoon you say he's coming?' asked Kate.

'I hope you don't mind?'

'It suits me perfectly. I'd planned to see the exhibition at the Hayward Gallery.'

Joanna hesitated, then came and sat on the edge of Kate's bed. 'I was rather hoping you'd stay.'

Kate studied the girl's crestfallen expression. 'Do you think that's wise?'

'Wise or not, I'd just feel a lot happier if you were around.'

'If it makes you happier, but should you decide otherwise . . .' Kate gave a small smile, 'I'll melt diplomatically away.'

It was late afternoon when the doorbell rang sharply

and despite her earlier show of calm an expression of panic crossed Joanna's face; Kate squeezed her arm encouragingly and went to answer the door. The once ebullient figure of Simon Forrest stood hesitant and awkward on the threshold.

'Hello, Simon.'

'Hello, Kate . . . Joanna . . .'

A small silence fell between the three of them and at Kate's suggestion they moved to the sitting room. She poured drinks for them all and the silence continued until she joined them.

'How are you, Simon?'

He spread his hands and attempted a smile. 'I'm all right . . . Kate tells me you've been in Paris, working?' Joanna nodded. 'I always said you had hidden talent.'

'You said a lot of things.' He made no answer. 'Then you always were a smooth talker. My problem was being too good a listener.' She spoke now with a perfect calm and her hands no longer shook.

'You're not making it easy for me.'

She threw him a scornful glance, then stood up and went to the window. 'What is it you want, Simon?'

His fingers tightened about his glass. 'I want you, Joanna. Want you back . . .'

'*I* never went away, remember?' She stayed looking out of the window. 'Why the sudden change of heart?'

'Not so sudden. I've been trying to locate you for weeks. No one had seen you or knew where you were living. I finally found out from someone who'd seen you at Nick Garret's.'

'You haven't answered my question.'

'Not having you made me realise just how much you meant to me. How much I really loved you.' He rolled his glass between his hands. 'I've been offered a job in South Africa.'

'South Africa!' exclaimed Joanna.

'I was hoping you'd come with me. That we could

start again. I know things could work out for us.' She turned away from the window and regarded him gravely with her dark eyes.

'And what if they don't?'

'This time they will, I promise.'

She was silent, thinking about it, then shook her head. 'It's too late, Simon.'

'Why too late?'

'You say that not having me made you realise how much I meant to you.'

'How much I *loved* you.'

She attempted a smile. 'Funny, that, because it made *me* realise just how *little* you meant to me.'

Her words appeared to stun him. 'You can't mean what you say!'

'Yes, I do, Simon.'

'If only you'd give me a chance, I know things could be as they were . . .'

'As they were?' Her voice had grown quiet. 'Is that what you're promising me? The endless waiting and wondering, the pain, the unbearable pain of not knowing, not wanting to know, and the utter despair of being left behind, alone? No, thank you.'

He shook his head forlornly. 'I don't blame you for being bitter.'

'Bitter!' Her voice was filled with contempt. 'Of course I'm bitter. One moment you're mouthing protestations of undying love and the next you're disappearing out of my life with a shrug and a full suitcase.'

'I had no choice,' Simon muttered.

'You had me. Wasn't that enough?'

'Don't you understand that losing my job meant losing my self-respect . . . How could I face you and expect you to feel the same about me?'

'How do you suppose I felt?' she retorted. 'Knowing that my own brother had caused your dismissal. Don't you suppose I felt any shame?'

A puzzled looked crossed his face. 'Chester never told you?'

'Told me? Told me what?' She sank into the nearest chair, her eyes holding his. 'What is it he should have told me?'

'The truth.'

'The truth?' Joanna queried.

'It wasn't Chester who arranged to see Sinclair, it was Sinclair who called to see your brother.' Simon considered a moment, then drained his glass. 'As a journalist with a popular newspaper I influenced a lot of people . . . a lot of people with a lot of money to spend. For better or worse, the right words from me could maybe guarantee a style's success and financial reward for the manufacturer concerned. You know that old adage about the pen being mightier than the sword—well, I learnt how to convert that might into hard cash.' He leant forward, holding his tumbler between his knees. 'At first it was simply a gesture of thanks from the manufacturer for a good editorial; a free lunch, a bottle of champagne, but then the lunch became an expensive dinner, and the bottle a crate. As their rewards increased, their demands also, until the whole thing got wildly out of control.'

'You accepted bribes?'

He nodded wearily. 'On occasion I'd introduce buyers to manufacturers and if an order was placed, I'd be paid accordingly, always in hard cash.'

'Why, Simon? Why?' whispered Joanna.

'How else do you suppose a country boy like myself could afford, even attract, a girl like you, the sister of a wealthy man?'

'That doesn't say much for me.'

'It wasn't your fault. You were born into a world where you took a certain style of living for granted.'

'But we led such a simple life, both of us. What on earth did you spend the money on?'

'Simple for you, I suppose: dinner at some fashionable Chelsea bistro, tickets for the opera, or was it the ballet, weekends at quaint hotels in the country ... Things you've always taken for granted, but nevertheless cost a lot of money ... a lot more than I was earning.'

'But I would have settled for less—a lot less. I loved you.'

'I couldn't take that risk. You were too important to me.' Simon shrugged. 'The pity of it was being found out. It wasn't hurting anyone. No one was out of pocket.'

'Being found out worries you more than having accepted the bribes?'

'In any competitive market it's the usual practice. Ever wondered about the motoring correspondent who gets a whopping discount on the latest model, the City editor with a profitable sideline in unit trusts. At the time of a recession half the people are busy conning the other half.'

'And you decided which side you'd prefer to be on.'

'Some of us can't afford to be on the wrong side.'

'Where does Chester come into this sordid tale?'

He stood up and moved restlessly about the room. 'A manufacturer with whom I had refused to have further dealings revealed our past arrangement to Sinclair. Sinclair knew I was engaged to you and as Chester was his good friend, he decided to acquaint him with the facts. He'd decided to call in the fraud squad and suggested to Chester that he warn you off me. Not knowing, of course, that he'd been trying to de precisely that for two long years.'

'What was Chester's reaction?'

He pursed his lips. 'Apparently your brother persuaded him otherwise. He told Sinclair to lay his cards on the table and ask for my resignation and not to take such drastic action.'

'Chester did you a good turn, then?'

'Ironic, isn't it? That in the end it was your brother who gave me a second chance, but you won't.'

Joanna shook her head decisively. 'It's no good, Simon. There's nothing left . . . nothing.'

He lurched forward and gripped her shoulders, his face disbelieving. 'I don't believe you! You must feel something. Why else did you agree to see me?'

She glanced across at Kate before she spoke. 'Because someone for whom I care a great deal insisted I did.'

Simon's hands dropped to his side. 'Another man?' She nodded. 'He must be pretty sure of you.'

'He wanted *me* to be sure.'

'And?'

'And now I am.'

Perplexed, he put his hand to his forehead. 'The one factor I never even considered . . . another man.'

'You supposed I'd always be there for the asking?' Joanna said scornfully.

'No, of course not. I just got used to your brother being the other man.' He laughed ruefully. 'I never should have left someone as pretty as you alone for so long . . . I won't forget you, Joanna.' He bent down and kissed her cheek, then turned and walked out.

For a long moment, Joanna just sat there, very still and silent and far away, then she smiled across at Kate.

'I feel like a very large, very stiff drink.'

'You deserve one,' said Kate, pouring out the requested medicine. 'You fought a hard fight.'

'A bloody battle, more likely!'

'There don't appear to be any wounds,' Kate observed.

'None that a large gin and tonic won't heal.' Joanna sighed deeply. 'I feel so drained.'

'Now, at least, you know the truth, and that can't be bad.'

'Just imagine, I could have spent the rest of my life thinking I'd lost something worthwhile. Joanna stared into her glass. 'It's quite sad to be left with no illusions. At least when he left me the first time around I had my dreams.'

'But this time his leaving was *your* decision.'

'I suppose Chester would say that was my first step towards adulthood,' Joanna mocked.

'Don't you think someone else would like to know your decision?' asked Kate solicitously.

'You mean Chester?'

'I mean Alain! He's probably sitting by his telephone this very minute.'

Joanna's face went very pink and she stood up quickly. 'Would you mind awfully, Kate, if I rang him now in Paris?'

'I'd mind if you didn't,' smiled Kate, pushing her gently in the direction of the hall.

Alain was everything Simon wasn't and that Joanna needed; a man of integrity and substance who, in the short time he had known her, had instilled in Joanna the confidence to handle a difficult situation with dignity and for her, at least, life would be a lot happier in the near future.

Judging it time to leave Joanna alone with her phone call, Kate collected her coat and quietly left the flat. She intended to walk through Hampstead Village and on to the Heath, but the fine drizzle grew steadily heavier and on impulse she hailed a passing taxi and gave Molly Cunningham's address.

Thirty minutes later she and Molly were sitting down to tea and chocolate cake.

'It's a bit late for Sunday tea, I know, but I couldn't let all this cooking go to waste,' Molly explained.

'You made it yourself?' said Kate, surprised. 'It's delicious!'

'My nephew was due to visit, but thank goodness he caught chickenpox.'

'Thank goodness?'

'You don't know my nephew, and besides,' Molly cut a second slice of cake for Kate, 'we wouldn't be enjoying ourselves now.' She poured them both a second cup of tea, then settled back against the cushions. 'Now suppose you tell me your real reason for "passing by" and let's get really cosy.'

Kate was pleased to confide in Molly and to tell her of Joanna's good news; of her meeting Alain and their mutual attraction, Joanna's subsequent visit to Paris, Simon's reappearance, and finally his visit that afternoon.

'His revelations must have come as quite a shock to Joanna,' said Molly.

'She took it a lot better than I thought she would. She seems to have done a lot of growing up these past few months.'

'That will be good news for Chester. Does he know about Simon's visit?'

'I suppose Joanna will tell him.'

'She ought to, and soon. She owes him that after all the worry and headaches she's caused him.'

'I'm not sure it's been entirely her fault,' mused Kate, toying with her spoon. 'Chester has acted in this whole affair with the finesse of a bull in a china shop. If he'd stayed discreetly in the background Simon may have quietly faded away—as it was, his embattled opposition threw them into each other's arms. Don't forget that until Sinclair approached him Chester had no tangible proof of Simon's guilt.'

Molly leant forward and meticulously tipped her cigarette ash into the ashtray. 'It wasn't his petty fiddling that worried Chester, so much as his track record with the ladies ... one in particular he married in Ireland.'

'*Married?*' gasped Kate.

'Oh, they're divorced now, but at the time it was a particularly messy one, involving one of our girls from Publicity.'

'Was his wife in the fashion business?'

Molly shook her head. 'As a bright and ambitious young man he worked for a local paper in Dublin; bright enough to know he wasn't that bright and ambitious enough to marry the boss's daughter instead. The marriage turned sour and he came to England.'

'What happened to the girl from Publicity?' asked Kate.

'Christina? She appeared one morning in tears, gave in her notice, then just disappeared. Apparently the poor girl had outlived her usefulness to Simon Forrest.'

'But what did Joanna think?'

'All this happened just before she appeared on the scene.'

'No wonder Chester was upset when his eye alighted on his sister!'

'I don't think he would have minded quite so much if Simon had been truthful about the past,' said Molly. 'After all, she's a big girl now and entitled to make her own decisions, but even to this day, she doesn't know about Simon's marriage.'

'Why didn't Chester tell her?' asked Kate.

'I think that deep down he wanted her to discover Simon's true worth for herself.'

'Knowing Joanna, she'd probably have accused him of making it all up anyway.' Kate sighed, still unable to take it all in. 'To think that all along Chester was right and I was so wrong!'

Molly regarded her thoughtfully. 'You still love him, don't you?'

Kate stared at her empty cup, holding back the tears. 'Is it that obvious?'

'Don't worry,' said Molly sympathetically, 'he doesn't know and I haven't told him.'

'It wouldn't make any difference if you did. It's Erika he's marrying.'

'Only because he *doesn't* know and *you* won't tell him.'

It was raining even harder when Kate left Molly, and she was pleased to reach her warm flat. Wet and tired, she showered and slipped into her robe; the gift Joanna and Alain had chosen especially for her. Although it fitted perfectly she could see at once what Joanna had meant about its risqué qualities, for the fabric clung to her shape in a way that left little to the imagination; certainly not an outfit to be worn indiscriminately. And in the present circumstances, alone now in her flat, the irony of the situation did not slip Kate's notice.

It was after midnight, but despite her weariness she was unable to think of sleep; there were still too many thoughts racing through her mind, too many questions still to be answered. She wandered into the kitchen to make herself a hot drink and it was then that she noticed a note propped up against the coffee jar and Joanna's familiar handwriting. Darling Alain is catching a night flight from Paris. I've gone to meet him. Don't worry and don't wait up. All my love, Joanna. There was a postscript. Thank you, my dearest Kate, for everything and especially for Alain. Kate smiled to herself; even at a distance Joanna's enthusiasm was infectious.

The flat seemed very still and quiet and she knew that in the months to come she would miss Joanna's chatty presence, but just then Kate needed to be alone and she welcomed the respite. She sat in the dark, listening to the rain beat incessantly against the windowpanes, and thought of the future that stretched greyly ahead, unable to shake off the sense of desolation that threatened to overwhelm her. With Joanna's happiness complete her last link with Chester had been severed, but even now she could not visualise her life without them . . . without him. The sharp ringing of the phone broke into her thoughts, but she didn't answer and after a while the ringing stopped.

She stood up restlessly and went to the window. Outside the night glistened black and wet and suddenly it all came back; the night in Paris when he had surprised her in the darkened room, his unexpected gentleness and concern, his love that had brought her alive. To think it would end like this! 'No,' she moaned, her inner resolve beginning to crumble, 'no . . .' but it was a pointless struggle and she cried as if her heart would break. Life for her had really only begun after she had met him; her tragedy was believing he had thought the same. Now she saw she had meant nothing to him, nothing at all. Their squalid hole-and-corner relationship had been doomed from the start. In time he would forget her . . . possibly had forgotten, but a part of her would never be the same.

She heard steps approaching the house and then the doorbell ring. Supposing Joanna to have forgotten her keys, Kate hurried to open the door and stepped back startled as Chester's anxious figure appeared in the doorway.

'I've been ringing all evening,' he said grimly.

'Joanna isn't here . . .' stammered Kate. 'She's gone to the airport.'

He caught her arm in a tight grasp and pushed her through to the sitting room. His large dark presence dwarfing the room. 'It's you I want to see.'

'Me?' Her eyes widened as she stared up at him, bewildered.

'Why did you lie to me, Kate? Why didn't you tell me the truth about you and Boivin?' She felt his fingers grip into her flesh and she winced. 'Why did you lead me to believe you and he were to be married?' His voice was strange and fierce and she turned away, afraid to look upon the man she loved. 'Tell me,' he stammered with fury, 'I must know!'

'Please, let me go . . . You're hurting!' She twisted out

of his hold and moved away. 'If you must know, Alain is going to marry Joanna.'

'I know that. Why else do you suppose I'm here?'

'Don't tell me you're against that love match, too? I was under the impression you rather liked Alain.'

Chester took a step forward. 'I hated the man! Hated him because he had you, and tonight when I learned about him and Joanna . . .'

'Joanna rang you?'

'Molly rang.'

His eyes held hers and she felt herself blush, certain that Molly had told him everything.

'Didn't you once warn me never to listen to office gossip?' she said, as casually as she could.

'Is it gossip, Kate?'

'I won't deny I enjoyed your attentions at the time. Paris and an attractive man—a dangerous combination, but not one I lost any sleep over.'

His face was pale and drawn beneath the stubble of beard, and her insides tied themselves in knots at the anguish in his eyes.

'I don't believe you, Kate.'

She shrugged. 'I took Erika's advice.'

'Erika?'

'She advised me against mixing business with pleasure.'

'And you listened to her?'

'You'd be amazed at what I learned listening to Erika. That you have a passion for the ladies, or was it the other way around? I can't remember . . .' Kate smiled sweetly. 'It wasn't that important.'

'You're right,' he interrupted, 'since I met you none of them have been important.'

'What about your engagement?' she queried.

'It became easier to let other women think I was engaged; it helped to explain my sudden disinterest in the opposite sex.'

'You appear to have quite a problem, wouldn't you say?'

'Dammit, Kate,' he shouted, 'you're my problem!'

His voice shook with such intensity that she stepped back, fearful of the power he still might hold over her.

'Leave me alone,' she implored. 'Please leave me alone . . .' But her voice lacked conviction and in one quick stride he had caught hold of her shoulders and forced her to look at him.

'Tell me you care nothing for me, then I'll leave you alone.' His eyes pleaded with her. 'Don't lie to me any more, Kate. I have to know.'

She opened her mouth as if to speak, but nothing came out, so great was the tumult inside her, but both of them knew there was only one answer. And now, face to face with the truth and the intensity of her feelings, she felt herself trembling beneath his touch, her heart pounding against her ribs. Then she remembered Erika; that in spite of what Chester had said he was engaged to her and nothing had really changed.

'What about Erika?' she asked faintly.

'What about her?'

'Isn't she in love with you?'

He laughed gently. 'The only person Erika loves is herself. The reason she latched on to me in the first place was in the hope of securing a lucrative consultancy with Bennett's, and now that she's been given Simon's old job, I've seen the last of her.'

'Are you sure?' she faltered, not daring to hope.

'I've always been sure,' he replied, his face intense, and then she was in his arms and his mouth was on hers and his kiss was long and passionate.

'God, I've missed you,' he muttered, as they drew apart at last.

She tilted her face to look at him. 'I thought you'd forgotten me.'

His arms tightened about her. 'I tried ... how I tried!'

'You always were obstinate,' she smiled, feeling a heady release after all that pain.

'Me? If it hadn't been for your stubbornness I wouldn't have suffered so much. Look at me, I'm a nervous wreck!'

She trailed her finger along his cheekbone. 'I think you're beautiful.'

'Have you missed me?' he asked.

'Every day since I last saw you.' She nuzzled his neck. 'Did you think of me?'

'About little else.' Chester bent down and gently kissed her eyelids. 'How much simpler life would be if I hadn't fallen in love!'

She laughed. 'And I might have been a very successful sportswear buyer, although I suppose there's still a chance ...'

'Never. As my wife you will stay home and have lots of babies.'

'What if I resist?' she teased.

An amused glint appeared in his eyes as he pulled her hips against his. 'I'm your boss, remember? You'll do as you're told.'

'Who's arguing?' she whispered.

His hands moved possessively about her waist and pressed her against him, and Erika and the rest were forgotten. All that mattered was to be in his arms, where she knew she would stay for the rest of her days. A sudden flash of lightning made her tremble and Chester bodily gathered her up and sat in a chair. He kissed her ear. 'Perhaps now I'll settle down to some work. One way and another you've been a terrible distraction.'

'Since Paris, you mean?'

'Since when I first saw you. Lust at first sight, you might say.'

Her colour deepened. 'But you were abominable to me!'

'Because you made me nervous . . . very nervous. Such an alluring young lady working for me, with brains, too. Now that is a dangerous combination.'

She kissed the corner of his mouth. 'I hope you're marrying me for my mind?'

'You,' he said, cupping her chin in his hand, 'have a very sexy mind.' She laughed softly and laid her face against his chest; feeling his heart pounding beneath his shirt. 'Forgetful, though.' She frowned. 'You never did give me your answer.'

'Answer?'

Then she remembered their night in Paris together, when he had spoken of love freely given and she had insisted on wearing her badge of respectability.

'Had you forgotten?' he asked, gently pushing her away to look into her eyes.

What he saw there was answer enough and his arms tightened about her as he kissed her moist tremulous lips. She kissed him back passionately, her heart bursting with love. Knowing now that she meant everything to him she was no longer afraid to show her sexuality and her body responded to his with abandon. She shook with pleasure as she felt his hands move possessively over her body, then slip inside her loosened robe and caress her breasts. Their passion for each other was inexhaustible and she surrendered her whole being to his.

He pushed her gently away. 'Any more of this and I'll be anticipating the wedding breakfast,' he said jerkily.

She smiled up at him as her fingers traced the bare skin about his waist. 'The bride won't be complaining.'

Chester stroked back her hair and lightly kissed her forehead. 'My darling Kate, I promise you, you won't have *any* complaints . . . I've a feeling you'll make me a very contented husband.'

'I'll do my best,' she smiled, moving in closer.

Harlequin® Plus

THE MUSIC OF MOZART

Mozart is considered by many to be the greatest musical genius of all time. Yet, after writing and performing music all his life, he died tragically, alone and impoverished.

Wolfgang Amadeus Mozart was born in 1756 in Salzburg, Austria. His father, Leopold, a well-known violinist and composer, taught his son how to play harpsichord at a very early age, and young Mozart performed his first piano recital when he was only three. By the time he was five, Mozart was composing music, and when he was six, his father took him to Munich and Vienna on his first concert tour. Soon Mozart was being commissioned by European royalty, including the Empress Maria Theresa of Austria, to write music for state weddings and church ceremonies.

In those days, composers earned their keep by working in the households of noblemen or wealthy clergymen. Mozart's patron for many years was the archbishop of Salzburg. But the archbishop was a spiteful and jealous man, refusing to allow Mozart to play for anyone else and forcing him to eat with the servants. Finally, in 1781, the archbishop was unspeakably rude to Mozart in public, and consequently the young musician resigned and moved to Vienna.

There, he met and fell in love with Constanze Weber, whom he married. But without a patron Mozart had terrible financial problems and fell heavily into debt. In 1791, at the age of thirty five, he became seriously ill and died, and was given only a pauper's burial.

Yet despite his brief life, Mozart left a magnificent legacy for future generations—hundreds of pieces of music, from brilliant symphonies to such famous operas as *The Marriage of Figaro* and *The Magic Flute*. Eminent music scholars have said that, with Mozart, European music reached its highest point of perfection.

Choose from this great selection of early Harlequins—books that let you escape to the wonderful world of romance!*

*Some of these book were originally published under different titles.

Relive a great love story...
with Harlequin Romances
Complete and mail this coupon today!

Harlequin Reader Service

In the U.S.A.
1440 South Priest Drive
Tempe, AZ 85281

In Canada
649 Ontario Street
Stratford, Ontario N5A 6W2

Please send me the following Harlequin Romance novels. I am enclosing my check or money order for $1.50 for each novel ordered, plus 75¢ to cover postage and handling.

☐ 982	☐ 1156	☐ 1180	☐ 1195	☐ 1221
☐ 984	☐ 1162	☐ 1181	☐ 1200	☐ 1222
☐ 1015	☐ 1168	☐ 1183	☐ 1203	☐ 1237
☐ 1048	☐ 1172	☐ 1184	☐ 1204	☐ 1238
☐ 1126	☐ 1173	☐ 1186	☐ 1214	☐ 1248
☐ 1151	☐ 1175	☐ 1187	☐ 1215	☐ 1314

Number of novels checked @ $1.50 each = $ _____

N.Y. and Ariz. residents add appropriate sales tax. $ _____

Postage and handling $ _____ .75

TOTAL $ _____

I enclose _____
(Please send check or money order. We cannot be responsible for cash sent through the mail.)

Prices subject to change without notice.

NAME _____
(Please Print)

ADDRESS _____
(APT. NO.)

CITY _____

STATE/PROV. _____

ZIP/POSTAL CODE _____

Offer expires October 31, 1983

30456000000